Willis Boyd Allen

Kelp

A Story of the Isles of Shoals

Willis Boyd Allen

Kelp
A Story of the Isles of Shoals

ISBN/EAN: 9783337407032

Printed in Europe, USA, Canada, Australia, Japan

Cover: Foto ©Andreas Hilbeck / pixelio.de

More available books at **www.hansebooks.com**

BOAT ADRIFT.

KELP

A Story of

THE ISLES OF SHOALS

BY

WILLIS BOYD ALLEN

AUTHOR OF " PINE CONES," " SILVER RAGS," " THE NORTHERN CROSS,"
" CHRISTMAS AT SURF POINT," " THE MOUNTAINEERS," ETC.

BOSTON
D. LOTHROP COMPANY, PUBLISHERS
FRANKLIN AND HAWLEY STREETS
1888

TO

HALLIE

WITH SUNNY MEMORIES OF

APPLEDORE

CONTENTS.

KELP.

CHAPTER I.

A MIDNIGHT ALARM.

"WAKE up! wake up!"

Tom Percival turned uneasily on his hot pillow, — it was the middle of a sultry night in June, — and was dropping off into a sounder nap than before, when a hand on his shoulder thoroughly roused him. It was his father who spoke.

"Wake up, Tom, and dress yourself as fast as possible. I've just got word that there's a fire in our block down-town, and I want you to go with me. Are you awake, my son?"

"Yes, father. I'll be with you in no time."

Tom sprang out of bed, and very nearly kept his promise. He found his father waiting for him in the front hall, and a minute later they were hurrying down the silent street toward the red light that filled the northern sky.

"How did you find out, father?" asked Tom, keeping up a rapid pace beside his grave companion.

"A messenger came, — from the watchman, I think. He went back immediately to help. There may be no real danger for our place; but there are valuable books and papers in the safe, and the risk is too great."

On reaching Tremont Street, they found men and boys running in the same direction. A hook-and-ladder, called out by the second alarm, which was even now clanging dolefully from steeple to steeple, passed them with a jangle and clatter.

"Hullo!" cried Tom suddenly, catching a boy of about his own age by the sleeve. "Going to the fire, Bert? — Father, this is Herbert Martin. He was in the first class with Ran, you know."

Mr. Percival nodded hastily, but was too anxious for the safety of his building and its contents to pay much attention to the boy.

The three kept on, side by side, faster than

ever. Presently they turned a corner, and there
was the fire!

A glance showed them, that, unless the department accomplished wonders, the whole block was
sure to go. It was built of granite, six stories
high; and the great storage warehouse of Percival,
Walton, & Co. occupied nearly one-half of it.
Huge masses of golden red smoke were rolling up
from the end of the block, and plainly working
their way toward the centre. The air was filled
with hoarse shouts from the firemen, and the dull
booming of the engines as they worked like mad
creatures to drown out their enemy. Under foot,
the street ran half-ankle-deep with muddy water,
and was veined with the swelling coils and lengths
of hose. Here and there a little fountain of spray
burst from a joint, deluging the crowd, and raising a great laugh. Close by the corner where
Tom was standing, a pair of horses, unharnessed
from their piece of apparatus, stood calmly waiting for the homeward trip. Every few moments
an engine would shriek for coal, — *one, two, three*
or more sharp whistles.

All these sights and sounds the boys drank in,

Percival, after one glance at the fire and the direction it was taking, pressed forward, the boys keeping close behind him.

Before he had advanced twenty feet, he was stopped by a rope, on the farther side of which a policeman walked to and fro, swinging his club with an indifferent air.

Mr. Percival stooped to pass under the obstruction, but the guardian in blue was there in an instant.

"Can't get through here. Keep back!" he said sharply, while some rough fellows in the crowd jeered.

Fortunately a lieutenant of police appeared at just the right moment, and the rich merchant beckoned to him hastily.

"Lieutenant, here is my card. The fire is working along toward my offices, and I have important papers there that must be got out."

"All right sir. I know your face," rejoined the officer, after one keen look. "You can pass," and he raised the rope slightly as he spoke.

The crowd murmured at this; and remarks not at all complimentary either to the policeman or

Mr. Percival were freely made, as the latter quickly gained the other side of the rope. Tom followed, and Bert would have done the same, had not the man with shining buttons sternly ordered him back.

Mr. Percival and Tom were both too much engrossed with their errand, and the exciting scene before them, to notice the boy's absence until it was too late to return.

"I'm sorry, " said Mr. Percival, when he discovered that Bert was not with them, " but there's no time to think about it now. We must' get into our building at once, Tom. I can see smoke coming out of the windows already."

"All right, father. Only I wish Martin had come along, to help carry the books, if we have to take them out."

To tell the truth, Tom was rather nervous, — not exactly scared, but he liked to keep very near his father ; and as they drew near the foot of the burning building, he reached out his hand, big fellow as he was, and got hold of his father's.

The scene was like that of a terrible battle, —an army scaling a lofty city wall, and beaten building a dozen ladders were planted at different angles. Some of these were just being settled into place; some the firemen were dragging away to a safer distance; one or two were actually ablaze near the top. The upper half of the opposite buildings, with dark figures running to and fro on top of them, were brilliantly lighted up by the conflagration, which was out of sight from the sidewalk below. Men shouted from ladders and roofs. Dripping helmets appeared in the very midst of black volumes of smoke, at open windows, and hoarse voices called to this or that hoseman, " Give us water, there! Play away, Thirteen!"

" *Play away, Thirteen!* PLAY AWAY, THIR-TEEN!" came the call echoing up the street; and presently the roar of steam and dull, rapid thud, coming from a distant engine, told that the stream was rushing toward the fire. The ladder nearest Tom was planted against the sill of a fourth-story window. Near the top clung two firemen, motionless as the ladder itself. They held the nozzle of a line of hose, from which a fierce stream of water poured incessantly through the third-story window, directly in upon the fire.

Every minute or two a vast cloud of yellowish-black smoke would roll out, and hide the men from view. When it drifted away, there they were again, clinging, stiff and motionless, to the ladder and the hose, enduring to the utmost of human strength.

A sharp order rang out near by. The men on the ladder bestirred themselves.

"Hold on, Twenty - one ! *Hold on, Twenty-one !*" came the cry.

Slowly the gallant two descended from their perilous post, lowering the line of hose, which now hung loosely from their hooks. Just as they reached the ground, a heavy slate came *scaling* down from the roof. It struck one of the men on the head, his helmet only half breaking the force of the blow. He dropped like a log. Half a dozen firemen caught him up. A couple of policemen were there almost as quickly, and bore the insensible man away to the hospital, while another took his place. The ladder was disengaged from the window-sill and planted against the building fifty feet farther down the street. The enemy was gaining.

In the midst of all the noise, the rolling smoke,

the muddy rivers of water, the booming of engines and shouts of firemen, two or three young men moved calmly from one important vantage-ground to another, now and then stopping to jot down notes in the small blank-book which each had in his pocket. These bright-looking, self-possessed fellows were reporters; and it is only by service like this, in the very fore-front of the battle, that we gain our reports in the morning paper, of the "disastrous conflagration" of the preceding night.

As our two friends picked their way along, one of the reporters looked at them sharply a moment, then stepped up with a brisk air, and touched the elder of the two on the shoulder.

"Ah, Mr. Percival," said he, pulling out his note-book, and fluttering the leaves over rapidly till he found his place, "sorry the fire's in your building. Looks as if the whole thing must go, doesn't it? In case it *should*, you know, where are you insured, and how much?"

Mr. Percival gave him a few figures, impatiently.

"Rebuild soon? Don't know? All right, sir. Thanks. I'm on the 'Herald,' you know. Good-night, sir."

THE "JOURNAL" REPORTER.

Mr. Percival was out of hearing by this time. Looking over his shoulder, Tom saw the reporter writing away in the note-book, using his knee as a desk.

They reached the familiar doorway, strange and unnatural in the flickering shadows. Two or three lines of hose stretched up the stairway, which was lighted by one or two gas-jets, shining dimly through a halo of smoke. A small cascade of water was already rippling down over the stairs from breaks in the hose somewhere above. Mr. Percival ran up one flight, with Tom close after him. There was no need to unlock the office-door, for the fireman's axe had already been there, and they entered readily. There lay the books and papers that Tom had often carelessly glanced at, as he ran in to see his father for a few minutes between school and home. Now it was like a nightmare.

"Father, I can't breathe: the smoke cho-okes me," gasped Tom. They both were coughing almost incessantly. Mr. Percival had the gas lighted by this time.

"Keep as near the floor as you can, Tom," he shouted. "There's really no danger at present.

The smoke comes in through the basement, but the fire's a hundred feet down street."

"What do you want to take out, father?"

"Every thing in the safe, if we can. The watchman has carried off every thing else of importance about the office."

He unlocked the safe with some difficulty, turning the combination knob to its fifties and seventy-fives, and threw open the heavy iron door, which formed part of the wall of the room.

"Here, Tom, pile them upon the table, so we can take our arms full when we leave."

There were ledgers, bank-books, check-books, and bundle after bundle of papers. Mr. Percival pulled them rapidly from their pigeon-holes, and tossed them to Tom, who placed them in convenient piles, ready to be seized at a moment's notice.

All this time the smoke was growing more and more dense, and the packages had to be found and selected in the safe more by touch than sight.

"Haven't we enough now, father?" gasped Tom, rubbing his streaming and smarting eyes. "I don't believe I can stand this much longer."

"Only two more, the most valuable of all. They are greenbacks amounting to five thousand dollars belonging to a friend. I just put them in here over night to oblige him, as it was after bank hours. Look out, my boy! Don't drop them" —

Mr. Percival did not finish his sentence. A thick, black pillar of smoke, denser and *hotter* than any that had come before, rolled in through the open door, and filled the room. It poured up through the cracks in the floor. It enveloped both father and son in its deadly folds.

Mr. Percival staggered to his feet. Thrusting the nearest packages into Tom's arms, and taking what he could grasp himself, he hurried toward the door, where a fireman met him, and almost dragged him from the place. Even before they were fairly out of the room, a red light played about one corner of the ceiling, and the window-glass came crashing before a heavy stream of water from the outside, that drenched them from head to foot.

They had not been gone thirty seconds when another figure darted into the room. He stooped to the floor, and groped round, calling loudly, "Tom! Mr. Percival! Are you here?"

The red light grew, and he could see through the smoke that no one else was in the office.

Crawling on his hands and knees, he was making the best of his way out, when he struck against two small bundles of papers lying on the floor.

"Ah," said Bert to himself, "these may be important, and they've dropped them in their hurry. Lucky I came, after all!"

He buttoned them up inside his jacket, and none too soon made his way down to the street.

He had not taken ten steps before he found himself in the grasp of a burly policeman.

"Let me go, will you?" he cried. "I want to find Mr. Percival, the owner of the building."

"Oh, you do, do you?" asked his captor in sneering tones, hustling him along to the ropes and through the crowd with little ceremony. "What's that you've got under your jacket? Out with it."

"It's two bundles of papers I found in Mr. Percival's office," explained Bert, drawing himself up as well as he could under the tight grasp of the officer. "I wish you'd let me go, so that I can take them to him."

The policeman coolly took possession of the parcels, and proceeded to march Bert along the street at a rapid rate.

"You can tell the lieutenant all about it," said he grimly. "I've seen fellows like you before, — saving property at a fire, for the sake of the owner. A precious Protective Department you are!"

Bert was highly indignant at this treatment, and felt half inclined to give a sudden twist and run. But a moment's reflection convinced him of the folly of the idea. Besides, he was confident that he could explain it all satisfactorily to the lieutenant at the station, and be allowed to go home to his mother and Susie, even if he had to leave the papers in charge of the police-men.

He accordingly said not another word, but walked silently along beside the man in blue coat and shining buttons. Fortunately it was so late at night that but few people were out.

The lieutenant was writing busily at his desk when Bert was brought in. Two or three officers lounged carelessly on the benches around the room, and a "Journal" reporter chatted with one of them about an affray that had taken place in North Street half an hour before.

Bert told his story simply and honestly, not even withholding his own name, though the reporter had pulled out his note-book, and was jotting down the item.

When he had finished, the boy looked up innocently to the lieutenant, fully expecting to be discharged.

"Give him No. 6," said the officer briefly, laying aside the parcels which he had been examining.

"Aren't you — won't you let me go now?" stammered Bert, a hot glow mounting to the roots of his hair.

The lieutenant did not even deign to reply.

"Pockets," he said tersely to the policeman who had made the arrest; and poor Bert was made to empty every pocket of its contents, which were placed under lock and key.

"This way," said the officer.

As Bert turned, he met the reporter's eye, half pitying, half quizzical. He was a young fellow, but had evidently seen a good deal of rough life, in his calling.

"Say," said Bert eagerly, "don't put my name in the paper, will you? It's all a mistake, from beginning to end."

"That's what they all say," remarked the reporter doubtfully. He seemed impressed, though, by the boy's frank face and manner.

"But think what a harm 'twould do me, and how badly you'd feel," pleaded Bert, "if it turned out to be true."

"Well, well," said the other good-naturedly, drawing his pencil across a line or two of his notes, "we'll see how you come out to-morrow. If you're fooling me, young fellow, this part will all have to go in next day."

Bert reached out his disengaged hand, and the reporter gave it a hearty grip.

"Hope you're all right, any way," said the latter. "You're too young to be in here," he added with the air of a veteran.

Five minutes later Bert was seated on his little iron bedstead in cell No. 6.

"I suppose I could have sent for Mr. Percival," he told the policeman; "but he may not have reached home yet, and it's only four hours to morning, any way. I may as well wait."

The man's steps echoed along the corridor, up the stone stairway, and ceased.

A poor drunken creature in the next cell sang half-crazy songs, while two or three other prisoners shouted at him to stop.

At last the place became quieter; and the boy, worn out with the exciting events of the night, fell asleep.

CHAPTER II.

C AN'T let you take away any thing to-night, sir," said a little dark-whiskered man, as Mr. Percival and Tom, half blinded by smoke, and dripping with water, rushed out of the burning building.

"These are important papers from my safe," said Mr. Percival hastily. "Ask the chief, or any policeman of rank, to identify me."

"I've no doubt it's all right, sir," replied the small man respectfully enough ; "but I can't stop to hunt up anybody now, and our rules are strict. Just place your bundles in the Protective wagon over here, and you shall have every thing safe in the morning. They shall be taken away and locked up at once."

There was no help for it ; and the three picked their way over writhing lines of hose, and be-tween pieces of apparatus, to the team of the

Protective Department, which was quietly waiting on the outskirts of the crowd.

Mr. Percival deposited his precious parcels and books, one by one, in a stout trunk that was kept for that purpose.

"Now, Tom," he said, turning rather nervously to the boy, "of course, you have the bills?"

"This is all I have, father," faltered Tom, turning pale. "I'm awfully afraid they — fell."

"O Tom, you *couldn't* have dropped them! Five thousand dollars!"

Tom buried his face in his hands, and was silent.

Mr. Percival turned toward the warehouse, as if about to rush in again; but the officer laid his hand kindly on his shoulder.

"It's no use, sir," said he. "The fire's above it, and is running all through the second floor. There go the streams in now, and there's fire leaking out through the window this minute. Sorry for you, sir. I'll make every inquiry. Good - by. — Warden," turning to the man in charge of the wagon, "drive off at once, and leave that trunkful of goods, claimed to be Mr. Percival's. Come back as soon as you can."

There was a rush backward in the crowd, as the horse turned sharply and galloped away with the wagon. The officer disappeared in the direction of the fire. The engines boomed more loudly than ever, and belched forth great showers of sparks, until each seemed a mimic conflagration. The light behind the windows of the warehouse office, and the smoke that rolled hotly out, told plainly that to enter it was no longer possible.

Mr. Percival, recovering his composure, turned quietly away.

"Come, Tom," he said in gentle tones, "we'll go home. The loss of the bills was really no more your fault than mine. I forgot them entirely, from the time I held them out to you, till we had left the building."

Leaving the uproar of the fire behind them, they walked up town through the quiet streets, and, weary and depressed, lay down once more in their beds, only to dream of blazing walls, and bundles of bank-bills scorching and shrivelling before their eyes.

As they afterward learned, the fire was confined to the building where it started. At about day-

light it was fairly under control, and only a couple
of engines remained to pour water on the steam-
ing ruins.

When the first ray of sunlight found its way
somehow through the grated windows of Station
D, and actually for a few minutes into cell No. 6
(for where will God's blessed sunshine not find
its way, sooner or later?), it rested on the rough
stones over the head of a sleeping boy; then
passed down, over the iron threshold, across the
grimy floor, and — oh, if the heart-sick prisoners
could have followed it ! — out once more through
the window. Having done what it was sent to
do, and brightened that place of gloom and
despair ·for a brief half-hour, as it had done
patiently day after day, year after year, ever since
the cells were built, it went its way. So, in advance
of the great, hot, healthy, life-giving sun, thousands of gentle rays dart forward, touching weary
foreheads, kissing rosy faces of sleeping children,
awakening drowsy birds for their matins, carrying
messages of hope and of coming day around the
world.

Bert Martin slept peacefully on, undisturbed
by his shy visitor, perhaps having sweeter and

sunnier dreams because it had flitted by. Once
or twice a broad-shouldered policeman passed the
grated door, and his grim mustache curled in a
kindly way as he noticed the boy's deep slumber.

At length an interruption came. A heavy door
clanged, and footsteps hastened down the stairs
and along the corridor.

"Bert, my dear boy!"

"I say, Bert, old fellow!"

Bert rubbed his eyes, as he sat up straight, and
tried to remember where he was.

"Bert!"

The door swung open, and a boyish figure
rushed in and threw itself into his arms.

Could it be Tom — and crying, too!

Then it all came back to him, — the fire, the
rescued parcels, the arrest and imprisonment.

"Have you got your papers, Mr. Percival," he
asked eagerly, giving Tom a re-assuring hug at
the same time.

Mr. Percival held up the bills.

"We'll talk about that by and by," said he
quietly, holding the boy's hand in a tight clasp.
"All I want now is to get you away from here.
I shall never forgive myself " —

"Oh, I don't mind it a bit!" said Bert eagerly, shaking himself into shape, and pushing back the hair from his eyes. "I knew you would make them understand, as soon as you found I was here. And mother and Susie didn't know when I went out last night. I was going to send word the first thing this morning."

In the office up-stairs his pocket articles were restored to him. The lieutenant reached over the desk, and shook hands with him.

"Mustn't blame me, my boy," said he, rather gruffly. "We gave you a good night's lodging, anyway. And five thousand dollars isn't honestly carried about by boys of your age every day."

"Five thousand dollars!" gasped Bert. "You don't mean" —

"Every cent of it," said Mr. Percival, smiling. "Come, boys, we must be off."

Just then Bert caught sight of a young man, indifferently scribbling on a scrap of paper, near the window.

"Oh, there's the reporter that was so kind last night!" he exclaimed, rushing over to him. "You see it's all right?" he added with a beaming face.

"Yes," said the "Journal" representative carelessly, but at the same time giving Bert's hand a good grip. "I thought I'd see you through it. Roused the old gentleman out pretty early," glancing at the clock, which indicated half past six, "but 'twouldn't do to let 'em cart you over to the Municipal. Get into the paper, sure, if they did."

"And did you really go away up there, and tell Mr. Percival?" Bert could have hugged him almost as hard as he had Tom.

"Oh, it's all right! Little scoop for the 'Journal,' you see. All in my line. It's in type by this time."

"Why, you haven't been near the newspaper-office since my friends came."

"Messenger-boy. Telegraph-station two blocks away. Going? Good-by."

On the way up town, Bert told them all about his adventures, beginning at the time when, after a dozen fruitless attempts, he had found a policeman who let him pass the lines, and had hurried directly to the business office to find the others. What happened after that, you know.

It should be added, that the actual money loss

to Mr. Percival by the fire was very small, both building and goods being well covered by insurance. A great deal of inconvenience resulted from the destruction of accounts, receipts, etc.; and years afterwards, when certain papers would be required, the clerks would be heard saying, "Oh, it must have been burned in the big fire!"

CHAPTER III.

A CHANGE OF PLANS.

ON a certain sultry afternoon, about a week after the fire, a group of young folks were gathered in the little arbor on the Arlington-street side of the Boston Public Garden, evidently engaged in a discussion of great interest to the whole party.

Only a few rods away the little curving pond lay beneath the sun's hot rays, as motionless as glass, save where a pair of stately swans made long, wavering carets in the water as they swam near the curbing. To the south the tower of the Providence Railroad station stood erect against blue sky and fluffy white clouds, its clock marking the hour of four. The wheels of drays and hacks and private carriages, rolling along Arlington Street or up into Commonwealth Avenue, had a hot sound. Everywhere along the garden paths was a yellow glare of sunlight, except under the denser masses of tree foliage, where the shadows made little grateful spots of coolness.

"Now, look here, Bess," remarked Tom Percival, who had hung himself over and along the arbor rail in an impossible sort of loop, "if you're going to throw cold water on this little scheme, you'd better stay at home."

"Cold water wouldn't be so bad, a day like this," said another boy, in a slow, deliberate way. "If you'd untie yourself, and sit down like a human being, instead of a chimpanzee, your remarks would carry more weight, Thomas," he added.

"I don't mean to throw cold water, Bert," said one of the girls quickly, while her brother straightened himself out with a discontented jerk, and dropped into a seat. "I only want to look at things just as they are. Tom is trying to get up this trip to Mount Desert, and we haven't even talked with father and mother about it."

"I suppose it would cost a great deal," added a sunny-haired girl, whom readers of the preceding volumes of this series would recognize is Pet Sibley. There were three or four others in the

IN THE PUBLIC GARDEN.

group, but they were busy talking over affairs of their own.

"What's all this about?" asked a voice that made them start with pleasure. "An indignation meeting, or a general court, or a debating society?"

"O Mr. Percival," cried two or three at once, "you're just the one we want to see!"

"Is that so? Then I'm glad I came home early from business to take Tom's mother out for a ride through Newton. What can I do for you?" He took one of the remaining seats, and looked around pleasantly.

"Father, we want awfully to go off somewhere together this summer, for a fortnight or so, — a regular gay time, I mean."

Mr. Percival's eyes opened wide.

"With nobody to take care of you?" he asked.

"Oh, of course we should have somebody older with us, sir! But we want to be all in one party."

"Have you selected a place?" inquired his father gravely.

"Well," Tom hesitated a little, "we thought of Bar Harbor. It's always jolly there" —

"Say 'I,' Tom," interposed Bess. "The rest of us never thought of going to such an expensive place, father. Some quiet little house at Kennebunk or on the South Shore would do just as well."

"I'm afraid," said Bert Martin, flushing a little, "that I — that I could hardly join the rest. My sister Susie could go, perhaps."

"Oh, you must, you must!" The girls all spoke at once, and then stopped awkwardly. They knew very well that Bert was poor, and that he and his people were proud, and would not accept a cent of money. Bert had gratefully — with tears in his eyes, indeed — but firmly declined any reward from Mr. Percival for his services at the fire, and the mortification of spending a night in the cell of a police-station. The rich merchant had been at his wits' end to discover how he could do something for the boy who had laid him under such heavy obligation.

As the young folks explained their plans, an idea seemed suddenly to strike him.

"I have a suggestion to make to this honorable council," said he solemnly. "Instead of Mount Desert, which is a good way off, and, as has been suggested by the member on my left, rather expensive for a party of six or eight, what do you say to a fortnight at the Isles of Shoals ? "

" Splendid ! " cried Pet, clapping her hands.

Tom looked up curiously, to see what lay behind this plan of his father's. Mr. Percival was very apt to have something " behind " his plans which proved the best part of all.

Bert's face wore a doubtful expression. He knew almost nothing of the fashionable seaside resorts, and could not tell whether " The Shoals " meant five dollars a day at a large hotel, or six dollars a week at a small one.

" Which house should we stop at ? " asked Bess eagerly; while Susie Martin, who sat next her brother, clasped her hands together nervously. It would be so lovely to be a whole fortnight with these nice girls, — and then the sea ! How she longed for it !

" The ' Appledore,' or the ' Oceanic ' ? " continued Bess, who had heard of these places from her friends, although she had never visited the Shoals.

" Neither."

" Neither, father ? Why, there are only two

hotels, unless you count that great barn of a boarding-house, on Smutty-Nose!"

"No, indeed! But there's still another island, and a house upon it, where we should be sure of accommodations. It's never crowded, I believe."

"What do you mean, father,—not Duck Island?" Tom's interest was increasing. "There's nothing on that but a shanty where they store lobster-pots."

"I mean," said Mr. Percival, rising, "that if you want to go, I'll see that all of our 'Pine Cones' set of young folks—including you and your sister now, Herbert: we can't spare you—are landed on Duck Island five days from now."

"Where could we sleep, sir?"

"The girls in the fisherman's hut, which is a fine, dry little affair, I assure you; the boys in a double-roofed wall tent pitched close beside the shanty. The only condition I make is that you take no servant, but do your own work,—fire-building, wood-gathering, cooking, and purveying. You shall be well provisioned, and have a good camping outfit. My brother and his wife will go with you, I think. You know Will meant to bring Eunice down to the Latin School exhibition, for Randolph's graduation; but they were disappointed. They wrote me last week that they thought of going to the seashore for a little while."

"But the expense?"

"I'll take care of that, Bert. It will be very small compared with hotel living. The tent and all the camp utensils will be good for use any time in the next dozen years. Good-by, boys. Talk it over together. Let me know the result of the vote to-night."

And Mr. Percival was gone, walking away toward Arlington Street.

What a hubbub arose! Of course, the young people were wildly excited. There was no doubt about the vote, which was put by Tom, and carried amid immense enthusiasm. Bert tried to mention his scruples, but the rest wouldn't listen to a word.

Tom capped the climax with a brilliant stroke.

"Say, old fellow," said he, "you really must come along, to help split wood and build fires. I mustn't work too hard. Doctor says it don't agree with my constitution. I want another fellow to do my share: don't care any thing about your *company*, you know."

"I'll go," said Bert, "just to make you earn your living for once, Tom Percival!"

With a shout and such a merry laugh all round, that even the bronzed features of George Washington, on his steed near by, seemed for the moment to relax, the group separated into twos and threes, and **sauntered up the avenue** toward home.

CHAPTER IV.

BY LAND AND SEA.

IT is needless to state that the next four days were busy ones. The camp utensils had to be selected, stores bought, letters hastily exchanged with the Laighton brothers, whom Mr. Percival had known for years, and who generously placed Duck Island at his disposal for a trifling sum.

At length the evening arrived when the whole Boston party met on the forward deck of the good steamer "Falmouth," bound for Portland.

I said the whole party. There was one exception. When the camping-party was made up, Tom put in a plea for his dog Sol.

"By night," quoth Thomas, "he can guard us. In the daytime he will amuse us. I want to teach him to swim, anyway. Say, father, you'll let Sol go, won't you?"

Sol accordingly joined the campers.

As he is to be in our company for the next two

weeks, it will hardly be necessary to describe him.
Suffice it to say that he received his name "Solomon" from a way he had of slowly winking one
eye, and looking you full in the face with the
other; at the same time cocking his head a little
on one side, — a proceeding which gave him an
appearance of unuttered and unutterable wisdom.
It was decreed that Solomon should be boxed up,
and sent, together with the rest of the baggage, to
Portsmouth.

The main body of the party took the Portland
boat the evening before, partly for the sake of the
sail down the harbor, — there was a full moon, —
and partly to meet uncle Will Percival and gentle
"Aunt Puss" at that city, and proceed southward
again in their company.

The great hawsers were cast off; the boat,
towering like a floating palace above the green
waters of the bay, began to tremble from stem to
stern. Slowly she swung round until she headed
down the bay, paused a moment to let a dingy
collier pass, with a vast hissing of steam, across
her bows, then started quietly and steadily on her
eastward course.

An hour later, all hands except Mr. Percival

were on deck watching the twinkling lights along the Nahant shore, and the quivering track of moonlight on the water.

It is time now to state clearly who are to compose the camping expedition : —

At home, Solomon.

In Portland, Mr. and Mrs. W. Percival.

On the "Falmouth," Mr. H. Percival, Tom Percival, Bess Percival, Kittie Percival, Pet Sibley, Bert Martin, Susie Martin.

It was arranged that Randolph Burton (Tom's cousin, you will remember) should join them on the island a few days later. He was now visiting a chum in Hartford, where the two spent a large portion of their time in discussing the relative merits of Harvard and Yale.

Mr. Henry Percival, Tom's father, would see them well started in camp, and return to Boston the following day, to complete negotiations with the insurance companies regarding his losses by the fire.

There you have them all.

"Tom," said Bert, after a long silence, "what do you mean to do when you get out of school?"

The two boys were stretched out on the benches along the rail of the steamer.

"Oh, take in Harvard, I guess!"

"What then, I mean?"

"I don't know," said Tom, glancing toward his father, who had joined the group, and was sitting near by. "Any thing that turns up. I've a great notion for travelling, Bert. I'd like to spend two or three years going to queer places like Iceland, Patagonia, Alaska, and that sort. There's time enough for a fellow to settle down, after he's had a little fun."

"Don't you have any idea what profession or business you'd take up, if you had your way?"

"I shall have my way fast enough," said the other, a little under his breath. "No, I don't know that I care for one thing more than another. What do *you* want to do, Bert?"

"I'd like to be a writer," replied Bert quietly. "Perhaps I should have to begin as a reporter, and I might choose in the end to be a journalist. But I'd rather write strong, helpful stories and articles."

"I didn't know but you'd be a minister," remarked Tom with a half laugh.

"I would like to be one, but I'm not fitted for it. As a writer, though, I shall have a tremendous congregation if I choose to preach. Think of it, Tom! They say every book has, on the average, five readers sooner or later. Then, if five thousand copies of a story of mine should be sold, I should be talking to twenty-five thousand people!"

"Have you — ah-h-h — practised writing any thing?" yawned Tom, gazing over toward the Salem lights on the western horizon.

"Not to be printed. I'm not going to try that yet. But I take all the pains I can with my letters, I keep a note-book of events, and I'm going to write a careful account of this trip of ours, day by day. If you're a good boy, Thomas, you shall look over my shoulder some time."

"Well — ow-wow-ow!" — remarked Tom, with another yawn, "it's a humdrum sort of life. I don't want to bother my head yet awhile with — Hullo! what's that, a sea-serpent?"

Both boys jumped up, and peered out over the waves, where some kind of a long, dark object was bobbing up and down. In half a minute it was far astern.

"Not the sea-serpent," laughed Mr. Percival, who had risen with the others, "but an uncommonly long spray of kelp."

"'Kelp'?"

"It's a kind of flat seaweed that grows on the ocean floor, sometimes reaching a length of fifty feet. Along our own coast it is a more modest plant, not often running more than twenty feet; at least in the pieces that are broken off by storms, and drift about like the one we just saw."

"Queer," said Tom musingly. "Just think of it, — drifting, drifting about, bound for nowhere in particular, and not especially anxious to get there."

"How strange the steamer must seem to it," added Mr. Percival, "as it ploughs by, aiming for just one port, and doing its grand best to reach it! 'Humdrum sort of a life,' the kelp probably says to itself."

Tom looked up at his father with a start. But Mr. Percival was gazing off over the water as innocently as if he were not bringing up Tom's own words against himself.

"I suppose it's sensible not to bother its head

about it," continued the merchant, in the same tone.

Then, suddenly changing his jesting manner, he laid his hand kindly on the boy's shoulder.

"Tom," said he, "that idle, drifting, useless sprig of kelp is a type of the career I overheard you describing to Bert. The course he has marked out for himself is the voyage of the 'Falmouth.' Think it over a little, my dear boy. Do you want to drift, or forge ahead by your own will, — nay, by the power of a greater and higher Will?"

Mr. Percival bared his head a moment, and looked up into the starlit heights of sky.

Then he spoke in lighter tones: "Kelp or steamer, Tom, you'll have to be one or the other," and left the young folks to themselves.

A few minutes later the girls went to their staterooms. Bert and Tom staid on deck until they passed the "Twin Lights" of Thatcher's Island, which had been gazing at them like fiery eyes for the last hour.

In the morning all of our friends were awakened by the noise of the steamer making a landing at Portland, and blowing off steam. They

went at once to the railroad station, which was
not far away, and entered the breakfast-room.

A sleepy, but pleasant looking girl waited upon
them.

"Seven beefsteaks," ordered Mr. Percival
gravely.

The girl seemed overcome, for a moment, by
such a tremendous order ; but recovering presently, she hastened away, returning before long
with re-enforcements. These consisted of two
more girls, each sleepy, and bearing a tray smoking with the good things heaped upon it.

Breakfast over, places were found on the train,
which was waiting on the track. Before the girls
were fairly settled, in came Bert and Tom, leading uncle Will and Mrs. Eunice Percival, and
executing as much of a war dance about them as
the width of the aisle would permit, by way of
welcome.

The ride to Portsmouth was uneventful. Of
course the young folks had a great deal of fun
over every incident of the journey. One of Tom's
performances met with special favor. This was
the replacing of the little bits of pasteboard which
the conductor clipped from his ticket. When that

gentleman came through the car a second time, he observed that most of the tickets had been properly punched. But there was Tom's, apparently as whole as ever, so deftly had the tiny pieces been fitted in. Accordingly he picked up the ticket, and, after a hasty glance, punched it six times more; thus giving it, as the owner gleefully remarked, the general appearance of mosquito netting.

In the Portsmouth depot they found all their boxes and bags awaiting them. A yelp from one of the former proclaimed poor Solomon's whereabouts, and the dog was at once released. How his tail did wag! It wasn't much of a tail for beauty, but no other dog could possibly have got in so many wags to the minute. At length he became calm enough, while Mr. Percival counted up his baggage, to sit down and watch the proceedings, with one eye shut, and a most expressive look of content and wisdom in the other.

"Let's walk to the landing," suggested Bess, on hearing that it was less than a quarter of a mile distant.

Walk they did, therefore, or rather run ; for Pet having challenged Bert Martin to a race, all six

started at full speed along the sidewalk, and
arrived at the wharf of the "Oceanic" in a state
of breathlessness, from running and laughing.
The race was a tie.

As soon as they were quiet enough to look
about them, they could not help exclaiming at the
beauty of the river which was sweeping past the
wharf, a strong ebb tide toward the sea. Over
beyond was the green Kittery shore. A boatman
put out from the distant bank, and headed his
wherry high up stream.

"He is really making for this wharf," explained
the courteous captain of the "Oceanic," pointing
to the boat, which, with its two slender black oars
swinging silently to and fro, Tom declared looked
like one of those light-footed little insects that
dance about over the surface of fresh-water ponds
and brooks.

Strange as it seemed, the man really did row
his boat up to the wharf where they stood.

"Look at the jelly-fish!" cried Kittie, "just
like those in Boston Harbor. See how fast
this one is moving, bending himself in and
out."

"Not much purpose there, but it's better than

being just kelp," observed Mr. Percival with a twinkle in his eye.

Tom had no time to reply, for just then the captain called out "All aboard!" and they hurried over the gangway to find comfortable places on the little steamer. The boys brought a lot of stools up in front of the pilot-house, and there the party established itself.

The "Oceanic," which was not much larger than a good-sized tug-boat, but was evidently built for rough seas, backed out from the wharf; a proceeding which caused Solomon to lift his ears, and survey the deck intently, as if he feared he was sitting on a volcano. He gave vent to his feeling by one short yelp, and then laid his head on Tom's knee.

"Poor old fellow," exclaimed that young man, in pitying tones. "His bark is on the sea."

"Going to endure his trials in dogged silence," added Bert.

"Has to," said Kittie. "Of course, he can't 'a tail unfold'; it's too short."

"Oh, paws, right here!" cried Bess; while Pet added demurely, "Perhaps we could go faster if his tail was a-waggin'."

There was a great shout at this; and Tom, who attempted to remark something about its making the dog a more *solemn* '*un* than ever, was suppressed.

Meanwhile the "Oceanic" was swinging rapidly down the river, with the aid of steam and tide. They passed the Navy Yard; and uncle Will, who was familiar with these waters, pointed out the hull of the veritable "Constitution."

"'Constitution' must and shall be preserved," sung out Tom.

On the right bank of the river lay the rambling little town of Newcastle, with its gray, weather-beaten houses. · There were strips of green turf in front of them, running to the brink of the low ledges that in many places form the shore. Picturesque old boats lay at their moorings, or crept slowly along shore; making the most of each eddy to circumvent the tide.

The tide, the tide! Eager, silent, sweeping them down toward the sea. Its waters were laden with strange relics of the paths it had trodden, or the freights it had borne. Here were wisps of new-mown hay, from the Newington meadows ; drift-wood, that had floated on the blue Mediterranean ; sea-weed, torn, perhaps, —

> " From Bermuda's reefs; from edges
> Of sunken ledges,
> In some far-off, bright Azore ;
> From Bahama and the dashing,
> Silver-flashing
> Surges of San Salvador."

Still onward swept the tide, bearing the bits of meadow-grass that Dorothy had flung out into its current; the stained and blackened splinters that had been softly touched by the waters of the harbor of Jaffa ; the kelp and dulse that had been lifted in the white surf ; the little, restless steamer, and the restless, joyous human lives upon its decks, — toward the great, silent, waiting ocean.

Past the Kittery shores; past the white spire and churchyard, where the elm boughs were waving so softly, and the sunbeams and birds and gentle winds, all eagerly repeating, "Shall never die, shall never die ; " past the old fort that stood bravely against oppression nearly two hundred years ago ; past rocky points where the waves idly rose and fell; past fish weirs and

nodding buoys, and vessels riding at anchor;
past the lighthouse, at last, and out upon the
heaving breast of the broad Atlantic.

"Oh, look, look!" cried Susie, pointing to the
eastward.

Miles away, on the very edge of the ocean, half
clouds, half dreams, two or three long light piles
of rock — or mist — heaped themselves against
the blue sky.

They were the Isles of Shoals.

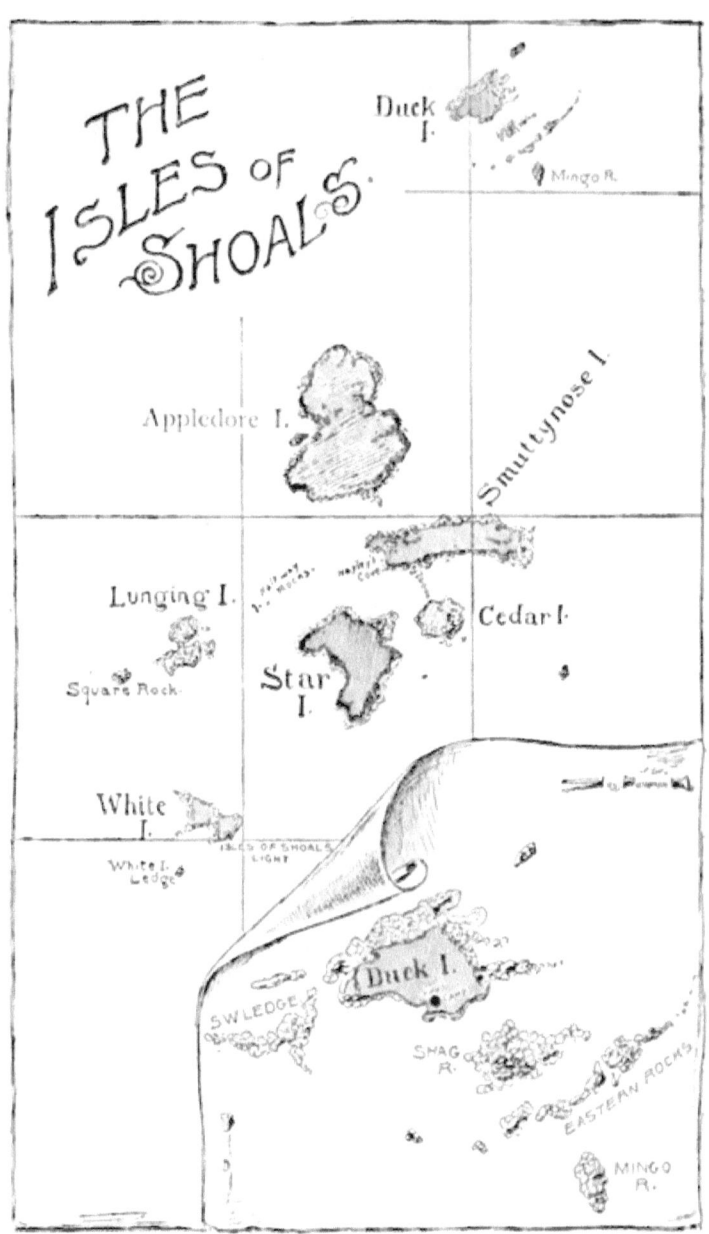

MAP OF ISLES OF SHOALS.

CHAPTER V.

CAMP KELP.

HALF an hour later, Mr. Percival reviewed his recruits upon the pier at Appledore.

"All here?" he said, counting rapidly. "Then let's go right up to the hotel, and get rooms for to-night. To-morrow we'll go into camp."

Quite a crowd of guests from the Appledore House had collected on the wharf to survey the newcomers, and welcome such friends as were to arrive by that boat. When all had come ashore, and the deck-hands were busily discharging the baggage, a long procession of men, women, and children moved slowly up the plank walk to the hotel.

The Percivals were received with cordial handclasps by Cedric and Oscar Laighton, the two brother landlords who have made these islands a delightful summer home to so many thousands of people, year after year.

A yellow-haired, brown-faced little girl of seven or eight years was sitting on a high stool inside the counter, and seemed to be waiting impatiently for the ceremony of receiving and registering the new guests to be over.

No sooner had Mr. Cedric finished "calling the mail," which he did with many queer twists and turns of the addresses, that kept his younger auditors in a gale of laughter, than his brother caught up the aforesaid little girl, placed her on his shoulder, and bade her, "Pull away, Dollie."

Dollie grasped a knotted rope that hung from the ceiling, and, with shrieks of glee, began to "pull away" with a will; while a heavy bell far overhead sent its jolly message of "Dinner ready" echoing over the island.

The Percival girls, with aunt Eunice, hurried up to their rooms, while the boys performed a hasty toilet in a small niche by the dining-room door.

"High old place, isn't it?" remarked Tom, groping for a towel after a plentiful spattering.

"Tip-top. What a dinner-bell! We'll hear it over on Duck Island."

"Wonder how they wake a feely row over morning?"

"Probably anchor the steamer off ther-tain-toot. Say, Tom, is my back hair all right.ing

"Just too lovely for any thing! Come on; father's ready."

The head waiter gave the party a table by themselves. Through the open window they could see gray rocks and bayberry bushes, and farther away a pink mist of wild-roses. A soft sound of waves came up from the rocks on the outer side of the island. There was a cool sea-breeze, as clean and sweet as a thousand leagues of salt sea could make it.

"I *know* we shall like it here!" exclaimed Kittie, as the waiting-girl hastened off to the kitchen with her tray. "Bess, I really caught a whiff of wild-rose then."

"And the bay,—isn't it delicious?"

The meal passed off merrily; and in the afternoon there was a walk over to the eastward rocks, where the waves were breaking in grand music. Hardly more than a mile away lay Duck Island, which was to be their home for two weeks.

A yellow-hair it looks as if the waves would or eight yeat over it," exclaimed Bess. "Not a the coun sight anywhere!"

for the can't see any house, either," said Tom, making a telescope of his hands.

"Here, Tom, take my glass. It's a little more powerful than yours," laughed Mr. Percival. "What do you see now?"

"I've found it, sir; a little gray hut, just the color of the rocks. My, what reefs!"

"Yes, they run out for half a mile from the island. Many a good ship must have gone to pieces on them. We shall have to navigate carefully when we row over there to-morrow. I hope it will be clear."

"What difference will that make, so long as it doesn't actually rain?"

"There's plenty of room to lose our way in, between Appledore and Duck, and there's always a long ground-swell rolling in from the outside. We won't start if there is any fog about."

All the afternoon they staid on the rocks, laughing, talking, watching the tide come in, and making plans. There were other parts of Appledore to explore; but they decided to take them another day, when they could easily row over from camp.

In the evening there was a musical entertainment in the parlor, given by a glee club of young collegians. Their songs, though not of the highest order of merit, were received with applause by the good-natured audience, who afterward contributed generously to a fund for the benefit of the performers.

Tired and sleepy, the Boston party climbed the steep stairs to their rooms at last, and were soon dreaming to their hearts' content. Tom and Bert shared one room. At seven o'clock next morning they were awakened by the sweet notes of a bugle sounding along the piazza beneath their window.

"It's the *réveille*," cried Tom, jumping out of bed, and running to the window. "Isn't that a jolly rousing-bell?"

"I see it appeals to your martial spirit, Thomas," yawned Bert. "I wish he'd bugle about half an hour later, though. I'm awfully sleepy."

"So'm I. Let's have forty more winks."

"Not much. Lucky I came along to play ant, thou sluggard!"

And Bert began to dress so vigorously that it fairly woke Tom up to see him.

As soon as breakfast was over, final preparations for camp began. The guests of the hotel — there were not many so early in the season — were extremely curious to learn all about this expedition; but the Percivals did not care to enlighten them as to every detail, preferring not to have too many visitors. As for the Laighton brothers, they considered it a splendid joke, and told the girls, with a laugh, that within forty-eight hours they'd all be back at the "Appledore," begging to be taken in. Whereat Pet squeezed Kittie's hand, and looked — a whole library.

" Come on," called the boys at length. " We're all ready to start."

" Father's waiting down at the wharf. Hurry up, girls," added Tom, fussing about, snatching up the wrong shawls, and carrying Pet's waterproof upside down, with the hood dragging. " Good-by, Mr. Laighton."

" Good-by, good-by." And, as they scampered down the plank walk, the big bell rang out loudly, while the bugler wound a merry blast from some distant out-building.

Aunt Puss was as excited as Solomon himself.

"Land!" said she, "it seems 's if I was a girl
again, going to a picnic. William, are you sure
you put in the tea, and the arnica, and the lemons,
and " —

"All in, mother," laughed uncle Will. "Anybody'd think we were off for the Azores, at the
very least."

"Glad you brought the lemons, auntie," said
Tom solemnly. "It may be a rough passage, you
know. If it is, we may have to batten down the
hatches and furl the jib-boom."

Mrs. Percival looked rather doubtful at this, but
concluded to leave matters of navigation to
experienced hands.

"Anyway," she remarked with quiet firmness,
"I'm not going to step my foot into a boat unless
there's plenty of life-preservers on board."

A diminutive steam yawl, called the "Pinafore,"
was moored to the wharf. It now called the party
together by three shrill whistles.

Boys, girls, and older people crowded on board,
while a goodly amount of baggage was stowed
fore and aft.

"Let go," called the captain — a handsome, sun-burned young fellow — to his crew.

"Ay, ay, sir!" responded the crew, like one man, — as indeed it was.

The captain took the wheel, and the crew sat down by the engine.

Puff, puff, puff, went the "Pinafore" out from the wharf, backward; then stopped to think a moment; then straight off, and presently headed due north-east.

At this moment, Mrs. Percival's apprehensions were excited by her discovery of two boats astern, in tow of the "Pinafore."

"What — what are they for?" she inquired timidly of the crew.

"Oh, those, ma'am, are to" —

"Escape in," interposed Tom, looking sadly off over the water.

The crew's smile broadened.

"To land in, ma'am. We can't get up close to the rocks in this boat, without risking the propeller. There won't be any trouble."

Was ever salt breeze so fresh and cool and sweet as that which just roughened the blue waves that morning between the two islands?

Susie Martin thought not ; as she sat on one of the cushioned seats inside the rail, and leaned far out, so as to watch the bubbling, dancing water dash away from the stanch little steamer's sides, and feel the rush of air upon her cheeks. Overhead a snow-white sea-gull floated, looking down at them with bright, curious eyes as they passed beneath him.

The moment they were beyond the shelter of Appledore, they felt the lift of the slow ocean swell. It was not enough, however, to seriously trouble any one on board ; and the trip seemed all too short, when the captain rang his bell for the engineer to stop, and soon after to back, until the " Pinafore " lay motionless upon the water, save for the gentle rise and fall of the waves.

" To the boats ! " shouted Mr. Percival cheerily.

The nearer of the two, which was a small cat-rigged sloop, was brought up alongside, and loaded with baggage. Mrs. Percival and uncle Will, with Pet, Susie, Kittie, and Bess followed ; while, last of all, the " crew " of the " Pinafore " jumped on board, and sitting in the stern sheets, sculled the boat off into the narrow passage between Duck Island and Shag Rock.

Mr. Percival and the boys immediately manned the other tow, which was a good-sized row-boat, and pulled slowly after the sloop.

A landing was effected at a point where the rocks fell off boldly; and, as it was high tide, even the ladies had hardly any trouble with the slippery seaweed, which would have been a serious obstacle at low water.

Boxes, bales, and bags were now handed ashore; the sloop anchored in deep water, in mid-channel; and the row-boat, after putting the engineer back on the "Pinafore," made fast by a long painter in a snug cove where she would not chafe.

"Good-by," called the party again, waving handkerchiefs and hats.

Toot, toot, toot! shrilly from the little steamer, which soon dwindled to a mere dot on the broad ocean.

"Hurrah!" cries Tom, capering about over the turf. "Alone on a desolate island. Now for camp."

It is a desolate island, indeed. Barely an eighth of a mile long, by thirty rods wide; rising not more than forty feet above the sea at its highest point, where the little group of campers is

gathered; boasting not a single tree, and hardly a
shrub, save wild-rose bushes and elder, but over-
grown by vetches and morning-glories, growing
lush and purple among the long grass, and in the
mimic ravines that furrow its surface; nothing
else but bare rock, and the eternal fringe of white
surf breaking lazily over the black ledges that
stretch away far out to the south-east, and cluster about the island on every side, — no wonder
it is the solitary, uninhabited island of the
group.

But neither Tom nor Bert nor the girls were
in any mood for moralizing. They scrambled
down toward the shore on the southern side of
the island, and presently a shout proclaimed that
they had found the hut.

It was a small, rudely built affair, but, as Mr.
Percival had said, snug and comfortable looking.
There was no lock on the door; and, lifting the
wooden latch, they entered.

"Lovely!" exclaimed Bess. "There couldn't
be a better place to live in for a fortnight."

The lobster-pots had all been cleared out, by
Mr. Percival's request, the day before. This left
a room of about fifteen by twelve feet, with two

windows on one side, a closet, and best of all, a fireplace.

"Oh, my! Do give me a broom," was aunt Puss's first exclamation, after one horrified glance at cobwebs and dust.

"Store's closed, ma'am," said Tom with a twinkle.

But uncle Will came in with a big bunch of elder twigs, which he proceeded to tie about the end of a piece of drift-wood.

"Not the best broom in the world, Eunice," said he, "but better than nothing. Perhaps rosebushes would do better."

"If I only had some hemlock or sweet fern!" lamented aunt Puss. "But never mind. This'll do first-rate to begin with." And dust commenced to fly so vigorously that the boys were glad to beat a retreat.

"I'm going down on the rocks and catch some cunners for dinner," called out Tom. "Come on, Bert."

"No you don't," interposed his father, giving him a good-natured shake. "Business before fish. We must get all our baggage down here, and the tent pitched, before anybody *thinks* of dinner."

Tom groaned, but set to work manfully with
the rest.

"Lucky we brought tent-poles," he remarked,
as these important articles were carried over
from the landing. "There'd be a poor show for
cutting 'em here."

By eleven o'clock the tent was pitched. It
had been hard work to find a level spot near the
hut large enough for their purpose; but it had
been accomplished at last. The hut was swept,
the tent showed its white canvas walls against the
blue sky, and from a short pole fluttered a small
American flag.

"Now, what shall we name our camp?" inquired uncle Will.

The girls looked mischievous as they consulted
together.

"If you please, sir," said Pet gravely, after a
few moments, "we would suggest, as a delicate
compliment to your nephew, the name 'Kelp.'"

Tom reddened, but joined in the laugh, and
presently shouted, —

"Three cheers, then, for CAMP KELP!"

And they were given with a will.

CHAPTER VI.

FIRST DAY IN CAMP.

A LL that afternoon there was work to do in
and about camp. Provisions were stowed
away in safe corners of the closet. The girls
improvised curtains out of shawls and pieces of
cotton cloth they had brought, "on general prin-
ciples," at uncle Will's suggestion. Bessie was
the discoverer of a tiny trap-door in the floor,
which, on being opened, disclosed a "delicious
little cellar!" Here the butter and condensed
milk, and such small quantity of fresh meat as
they had brought, were placed.

Meanwhile Mr. Percival put himself at the head
of a grand exploring and wood-procuring expedition, comprising all the masculine elements of the
party.

Passing to the rear of the hut, they clambered
across a small ravine, and struck off along the
edge of the cliffs, giving a look at their boats as

they passed. The tide was now going out; and the shores were everywhere fringed with dark masses of rock-weed, rising and falling with the swell that came in through the channel. A couple of hundred feet beyond rose the bleached ledges of Shag Rock, with not a green leaf or blade upon it.

The ebb-tide left exposed a host of smaller islands, grouped around the larger masses of rock. Beyond Shag, and on the outside of the whole cluster, they could just see the rounded shape of Mingo, with now and then a dash of white rising above it from the never-ceasing surf that growls around its rugged sides in the calmest summer day.

"I've heard it said," remarked Mr. Percival, "that no girl or woman ever set foot on Mingo. The duck-hunters land there sometimes in the fall; but it's extremely dangerous except in the smoothest water, and on the lee side."

"You tell Captain Bess that, and there'll be *one* girl on Mingo before many days," sung out Tom.

"Look at the gulls," exclaimed Bert, pointing ahead.

The north-eastern extremity of Duck Island
runs out into a long line of sunken ledges,
covered at high tide.

On these rocks, their snowy plumage showing
brightly against the dark rock-weed, were gathered dozens of sea-birds. As Bert spoke, one
of them spread his broad wings, poised a moment
like a boat with sails set, then rose softly, and
sailed away, followed by every gull in the flock.
It was a beautiful sight, and not one of the
explorers spoke until the last white wing van-
ished.   Then Tom the irrepressible awoke to
the purpose of the expedition.

"There's a lot of drift-wood in that cove,"
he remarked, scrambling down over the rocks.
"Come on, Bert. Let's get a good armful,
and bring it up here, and make a big pile."

. The two threw up slabs and tarry fragments
of plank and hewn ends of joist, while Mr.
Percival and his brother gathered them into a
heap. In ten minutes uncle Will called out
that there was enough for that night and the
next morning. Without exploring the rest of
the island, each took an armful of wood; and the
procession retraced its steps toward camp.

Tom had chosen a parallel path, a few rods from the rest. Suddenly he called out, "Bert, come over here. A bird just flew up."

"A sandpiper," said Mr. Percival, who had noticed the quick flutter of wings. "Her nest must be near here somewhere."

"Here it is," sung out Bert, after a few minutes' hunt. "Four eggs in it."

It was a pretty sight, — the four spotted, queer-shaped eggs lying in their snug resting-place in a tussock of grass. A corner of granite protected the nest from too much wind or sun. The boys left it undisturbed, and hurried down to tell the girls of their discovery.

"Supper's almost ready," called Kittie, from the door of the hut.

Supper! It seemed hardly an hour since dinner. But the boys came trooping in, willingly enough, for their first camp-meal.

There had been enough wood scattered about on a little rocky beach just in front of the camp, for cooking purposes. As there were no fish caught, and aunt Puss's experienced eye had guided operations at the fireplace, the supper was not especially barbarous. There was a piece of steak, smoky and delicious, from the drift-wood coals ; boiled potatoes, and " warmed over " bread, with tea for those who preferred it to water.

But I've not told you yet how they managed about water; for there's not a drop on Duck Island, except the generous tides of the salt sea itself. The boys had brought with them a tight water-butt, not half full of water. It was agreed that they should row over to Appledore at least once a day, during their stay in camp, and replenish the supply. There was a half-barrel, with a good tight bung, which they used for this purpose.

In addition to this, Mr. Percival had brought in the sloop a couple of large cakes of ice, which were carefully stored down cellar, with a plentiful covering of sawdust. As ice was plenty in the ice-house at Star Island, this commodity, too, could be resupplied as fast as needed.

After the dishes were cleared away from the pieces of plank, which, supported on two lobster-cars, had served for a table, the campers gathered around their fire to talk over the events of the day, and plan for the future. The boys threw themselves down on the floor ; and the girls, with

Mrs. Percival, found seats on boxes and blocks of wood saved for that purpose. As a raw east wind had sprung up at sunset, the drift-wood fire in the old fireplace was far from uncomfortable.

"I tell you what," observed Tom, stretching out his legs with a long sigh of content, and fixing his eyes on the dancing flames, "this is really — high!"

"What a delicious salty smell the whole place has!" said Susie, sniffing rapturously.

"It's the sea-turn," remarked uncle Will, who had just come in from an observation on the rocks. "The breeze has freshened up from the east, and there's quite a little sea running through the channel."

"Are the boats safe, Will?" inquired Mr. Percival.

"As far as I can see, they'll ride easily. I paid out the painter of the row-boat a little. The wind and tide set her right off from that point, so she's all right. The sloop rides like a duck."

"Hark!" exclaimed two of the girls at the same moment. "What's that noise?"

It was a dull, booming sound, repeated at irregular intervals.

"Only the surf, over on the windward side of the island," said uncle Will, after listening a moment. "The breakers are coming in with the tide. It isn't going to blow hard. This sea-turn often comes up after a hot day in shore."

There was another pause, broken only by the dull roar of the surf, and the crackling of the fire.

"Have there ever been any wrecks on this island, I wonder?" Pet shuddered a little as she asked the question.

"A great many, I am afraid. Some noble vessels have gone ashore on these terrible ledges within a very few years. Whenever there is a storm, the sea runs fearfully high on all these low islands. I've often stood on the eastern rocks at Appledore, and watched the waves breaking right over Shag and Mingo."

"To-morrow," added Mr. Percival, "perhaps we can go over to New Hampshire and see the surf. It is very fine there after an easterly storm."

"New Hampshire? Why, father," said Bess, looking puzzled, "we don't want to go ashore so soon, do we? It would take so long to sail nine miles and back."

" The boys can row you to New Hampshire in twenty minutes," said Mr. Percival, laughing at Bessie's bewilderment.

" I don't see how."

" We are now in Maine. Appledore and Smutty-Nose are in the same State. But Star Island, White, Cedar, and Malaga are in New Hampshire."

" How funny! I don't see what difference it makes, anyway."

" It made so much difference, some two centuries ago, that a whole townful of people left Appledore, or Hog Island as it was then called, and moved to Star."

" What was that for, Mr. Percival?" asked Bert, much interested.

" Why, there was a thriving town of six hundred inhabitants, in those days, on the southern end of Appledore. I'll tell you more about it, or your uncle will, when we explore that island. In 1679, or thereabouts, the good people of this town of 'Appledoore' concluded that the Massachusetts taxes were too high for them, and, leaving that island like the gulls we saw this afternoon, settled on Star, half a mile away, forming the new town of Gosport."

"But there's no town of Gosport now?"

"No, Kittie. That, too, has disappeared, within my memory. It is only a few years since I walked up the steep, crooked little streets among the fishermen's houses, gray and crumbling, and patched with yellow lichen like the ledges they were built on. Now there is hardly a vestige of them left. The old parsonage is there, and the little meeting-house; but the new hotel stands like Aladdin's palace, built up in a night, where the lights of Gosport once twinkled, and the women waited for their husbands who were at sea."

"Now, girls," broke in aunt Puss briskly, "it's time to go to bed. Boys, good-night. Sorry to have you leave us; but I'm tired 's I can be, and Susie's been working like a beaver all the afternoon, — and the rest, too, for that matter."

"Good-night, good-night," the boys called out, as they passed through the door. "Don't forget to remember what you dream. First night in a new place, you know."

A couple of mattresses had formed a part of the baggage. These were left in the hut, together with a large bag of ticking, now filled with straw.

The boys had plenty of clean straw in their

tent, which, with the lantern hanging overhead, and boxes ranged around the sides, wore a wild and lawless aspect such as delighted their very hearts.

Besides, they had one immense advantage over the girls, at night; at least, so Tom considered it. They had Solomon.

The lantern was extinguished; the campers all curled up in the straw, which had a good plank floor under it. Solomon was sleepy like the rest, and, having gravely turned round three or four times, laid himself down and snuggled up as near Tom as possible.

Now and then they could hear a merry laugh from the neighboring hut; but at length that pleasant sound ceased, and nothing was heard but the quiet breathing of the sea, as the tide crept in around the rocks, and up the little pebbly beach below.

CHAPTER VII.

WHITE ISLAND.

BEFORE sunrise next morning, both boys were wide awake, and creeping out of the tent. They managed to make their escape without disturbing either of the two older campers, and hurried down to the rocks where the row-boat was moored.

"Pull her in, Tom," called Bert cautiously. "Here's the half-barrel; look out, — put it up in the bows, where it will rest easy."

"All right," sings out Tom. "Jump in yourself. I'll row over, and you row back."

Bert's eyes twinkled, but he did not object. Tom pulled a good oar, and away they went, foaming through the water in splendid style. As they passed the end of the island, a song sparrow wished them good-morning cheerily enough from the top of a bayberry bush.

They reached Appledore safely, filled their

cask, and started on the return trip. When they were about half-way over, they noticed a sloop bearing down toward their island. It was filled with young men in regular yachting costume ; and one of them stood in the bows, pointing out the camp to a gentleman who seemed in charge of the party.

"Seems to me," said Bert, resting on his oars a minute, and scanning the little yacht and her crew, "that I've seen that fellow somewhere."

"Which one ? The sun's in my eyes so I can't see."

"That tallish chap by the mast. Why " —

Without another word he began to row vigorously toward the other boat, so as to bring the wherry nearly in her path. .

"Hallo, there ! Where you going ? Keep off !" called out two or three voices from the sloop.

Bert backed water so as to hold his position, and swung his cap.

"Hooray !" shouted the tall boy from the mast. " How are you, Martin ? Tom, old fellow, is that you, working hard, as usual ? "

Tom sat up straight in the stern ; and a look of delight gradually spread over his face as the other craft came up gracefully into the wind, and lost her way.

"Randolph! Where in the world did *you* come from?"

"Let me aboard, will you? I'll tell you all about it afterward."

He flung a small carpet-bag into the wherry, and, not without some difficulty, followed it himself.

"Won't your friends make us a call?" asked Bert hurriedly, as the larger boat filled away again to the south.

"No: they can't wait. They're off on a day's cruise, from the 'Wentworth.' My chum is there, on the starboard side, forward, — see him waving his cap? — and he was good enough to get his party to put me out on Duck Island. They came to Newcastle yesterday: so you see I got here earlier than I expected."

"That's jolly!" exclaimed Tom, surveying Randolph with round eyes.

"Don't look me over as if I was a seal or a porpoise you'd got aboard," laughed Randolph, "but tell me how you got here, and how you all are. Susie's here, of course, Bert?"

"ONE OF THEM STOOD IN THE BOWS."

"All here, and all happy," returned the oars-
man, pulling lustily toward Duck. "See, they've
started the fire for breakfast already."

"And there's Solomon down on the rocks,"
added Tom. "If he isn't careful, he'll wag himself off."

Just then two of the girls appeared beside the
dog. They scrutinized the boat sharply, and
evidently were puzzled to see three boys there
instead of two. Randolph drew his head down
between his shoulders, so as to conceal his
identity as long as possible.

"Look at 'em pat their back hair," cried Tom.
"They think we're bringing a fashionable caller.
Oh, my, there they go! No looking-glass down
on the rocks!"

"Tom, you're a rascal," said Randolph.
"Hall-o-o-o! Bessie! Pet!"

"Hove to!" commented Tom with a nautical
air. "I thought that would stop 'em."

Bess and Pet, having now discovered who the
newcomer was, waved their handkerchiefs in
great excitement, and presently aunt Puss came
clambering up to see what was the matter.

"Anybody'd think I was a prodigal son," said

Randolph. "I haven't done any thing *very* wicked since I left home."

He jumped ashore, helped the boys get up their cask of fresh water, and behaved as modestly as a young Harvard freshman of seventeen could be expected to under the circumstances.

"Now," said uncle Will, as the whole company rose from breakfast an hour later, "what shall we do to-day?"

"Clear away the breakfast dishes the first thing," remarked aunt Puss, setting the example by piling the plates up vigorously.

The boys and girls took hold with a will.

"Start a song, somebody," suggested Kittie; and Randolph at once led off with "Nancy Lee," in which the rest joined at the tops of their voices. With everybody working hard, it was scarcely fifteen minutes before dishes were washed, wiped, and put away, and every trace of breakfast removed.

"There," said Mrs. Percival complacently, "*now* you can plan for the rest of the forenoon."

"What do you say to a visit to the light-house on White Island?" suggested Mr. Percival, who,

"THEY DASHED AWAY, OVER THE WAVES."

to every one's delight, had decided to spend one more day with them.

"Just the thing. How shall we go?"

"Oh, a part in the sloop, and a part in the row-boat, if you prefer! The sea is so smooth there's no danger."

Mrs. Percival and Susie concluded to stay behind. The latter was greatly interested in seaweeds, and wanted to begin a collection at once. "It will be a good quiet time," she con-fided to the older lady, "when those boys are out of the way."

The light-house party was divided, as had been suggested. Randolph, Pet, Kittie, and Bess took the smaller boat, and the rest went in the sloop.

"What a glorious morning for boating!" said Pet, as they dashed away over the waves. "Don't pull too hard, Randolph. Bess and I are going to take your places rowing when you and Kit are tired."

Kittie laughed at the idea, but before they were half-way to White Island was glad to yield her oar to the other. Although the wind was light, the little choppy waves and the long swell made rowing seem very different from the fresh-water exercise she was accustomed to in the summer.

In the course of half an hour they reached the little bay that lies between the two curving shores of White Island and Scavey's. A huge mass of rock, as high as a three-story house, towered above them on the left.

"That's White Island Head," said Randolph. "The fellows pointed it out to me this morning. There's always more or less surf running on the point. Look at that breaker."

The sail-boat was anchored just outside the bay, her crew having evidently gone ashore in the lightkeeper's boat.

"Come on," shouted a man who stood waiting on the rocky beach just ahead.

As Randolph, now taking both oars, pulled cautiously toward him, the man called out again, —

"Fetch her up on the ways. Head right between 'em."

It was rather a ticklish job for a landsman. The "ways" were a couple of greased beams, bolted down to the rocks about a yard apart, and extending up out of the water into a boat-house. Randolph did his best; but when he was about twenty feet from the ends of the beams, a wave came rolling in from outside, swinging the boat around broadside on, in spite of his utmost efforts. In another moment she would have struck and capsized, had not the light-keeper dashed into the water up to his knees, and shouting, "Back your port oar! Back water!" seized the nose of the boat, and by main strength, aided by Randolph's desperate strokes, brought it round and between the ways, which held it steady.

"There," said the man quietly, as if nothing whatever had happened, "now sit right where you are, and we'll haul you up a bit."

Whereupon he called to a young fellow who was working near by; and the two, hooking a hawser on the bow of the boat, and turning a windlass in the boat-house, pulled up wherry, passengers, and all, high and dry upon the ways.

The girls looked a little pale as they stepped over the gunwale, and tiptoed up the slippery beams.

"I did think we were going to get dreadfully wet," confided Kittie to Pet.

"I know; but don't say much about it, or Randolph will feel hurt," said wise Pet.

So they were soon laughing again, and racing up the long wooden passageway to the light-house, where they overtook the sail-boat party, who had been waiting for them.

"This is the lower story of the old light-house," explained uncle Will, pointing out the deep window-seats, that looked like embrasures in a fort.

"Oh, I know!" said Bess. "Mrs. Celia Thaxter used to live here when she was a little girl. She tells about it in that lovely book I brought with me, 'Among the Isles of Shoals.' Don't you remember how she says she played in the covered walk on stormy days, and sometimes used to light the lamps herself?"

"She has lighted a good many lamps since, in her beautiful poems," said Mr. Percival quietly. "I think that might be another name for poets, — 'lamp-lighters.'"

"Or light-house keepers," added Bess.

Bert Martin said nothing, but the words strengthened his resolve to spend his life, so far as he could, in writing noble and strong words, that should shine in the world, and help people like sunshine by day, and the gleam of the light-house in night and storm.

Slowly the little party crept up over the winding stairway.

"Here is the machinery that makes the light revolve," said the courteous light-keeper, setting it in motion. "It's very nicely adjusted, so that a pin placed in the track of that lower brass wheel would stop the whole affair."

"Oh, *do* try, sir!" Two of the girls had each a pin out of her belt before you could wink.

"One at a time," good-naturedly. "There."

Sure enough, the beautiful creature of polished brass glided gently around until it reached the pin, trembled for a moment, and stood still.

"I shall have to help it a bit," said the man, smiling.

With which help the wheel went on its way; and the light-keeper handed Bessie her pin, prettily flattened in the centre.

Of course Kittie and Pet had to have their pins flattened in precisely the same way, with mutual vows to keep them through life to remember White Island Light by. (Pet lost hers before night; Bess dropped hers overboard the next day; and the third — well, I heard Kittie complaining, not long since, that her "dear little flat pin was *somewhere* in her great haystack of a house, but in just what particular bunch of hay, she was sure she didn't know.")

But to come back to the light-house. They crept up the last curve of the stairs, and out upon the narrow iron rim that surrounds the base of the lantern.

Kittie gave one look, and hurried in again, declaring "she should jump if she staid out there another minute."

The rest clung to the slight rail, and looked out over the sea. Far, far below, the waves rolled in lazily, one by one, foaming among the crevices of the rocks. Nine miles away to the west and north-west, the dark line of the mainland rose against the sky. To the north-east lay the group of islands; and beyond them, faintly rising from the gray-blue ocean, the shaft of Boone Island Light.

"Why, here is another piece of this island," exclaimed Bess, as they crept timidly round to the other side of the tower, "with water between. The island is shaped just like a dumb-bell."

"That must be where the 'little dun cow' was," said Pet. "Oh, how lonely it must have been for a little girl!"

They completed the circuit of the tower, and were all rather glad, if truth be told, to get inside again. Down they went, laughing at the mildest of witticisms, and screaming (the girls) at the tiniest of dangers, until they were out in the sunshine again.

"All aboard!" called Mr. Percival, leading the way to the shore, after the party had registered in the visitors' book, in the pretty parlor of the light-keeper's house.

The girls followed the rest down over the beach. Uncle Will caught Pet's wistful glance toward the sloop.

"Want to go home under canvas, girls?" he asked.

"Well," admitted Kittie thoughtfully, "it was *real fun* rowing over, and I just's lieve's row back; but "—

"Oh, give in, Kit!" teased her brother. "You might just's well. Your hand's all blistered now."

"If you say much more, Thomas," remarked Randolph sternly, "you'll have to row back alone in the wherry."

"Oh, wherry well!" began Tom, but was suppressed at that point.

It ended in the whole party going in the sloop, with the smaller boat in tow.

"Let's go outside," suggested uncle Will, as he took the tiller, after the anchor had been drawn up and stowed forward. "The wind is about south-east. We can run off two or three miles, and then home with a fair breeze."

The young people all agreed to this; and the sloop, gathering way as it passed out of the shelter of White Island Head, careened merrily before the stiff breeze that had sprung up during the last hour.

"Now, a good, rousing song," called out Mr. Percival. And with Pet Sibley's clear, sweet soprano leading, they sang air after air, all taking part with a will.

That is, all but one. Tom gradually sang less and less, and at length ceased altogether. ·He sat on the middle thwart, well up to the windward rail, and gazed steadfastly ahead. He was pale, and he was silent.

"Tom," said Randolph, who could not resist poking fun at his cousin, "let's you and I go forward, and sit up by the bowsprit, where there's a jolly motion, — regular see-saw."

Tom's gaze grew more fixed. He did not move.

"Come, Tom," continued his tormentor, "give us a song. What was that comic thing you used to sing at recess up in the hall, — 'Bacon and Greens,' or something like that?"

Tom cast a look at Randolph that threw the girls into convulsions of laughter, but which was so irresistible in its appeal for mercy, that he was let alone.

"It's really getting a little rough out here," said Mr. Percival, holding on to the rail with one hand, and his hat with the other. "Don't you think you'd better jibe, Will?"

"Not with this breeze and big sail. I'll tack, and come round slowly. Look out for your heads, girls. Here she comes! All right, boom's over. Now, we'll be in quieter water, under the lee of Smutty-Nose, in five minutes."

The wind was almost directly astern, and the boat dashed along as if it had wings, not making nearly as much commotion in the water as before, but in reality going much faster.

Tom's courage returned, and his voice was once more heard.

As they drew near Duck Island, they espied

somebody on its highest point, waving a hand-kerchief vigorously.

"That must be Eunice," said uncle Will. "Either she's uncommonly glad to have us home again, or something's happened. Haul in your sheet, Henry."

This move brought them up to the mouth of the channel, into the smooth waters of which the sloop glided gracefully.

"Oh, hurry, hurry!" screamed aunt Puss, as they came within hearing. "She'll be drowned, she'll be drowned!"

"Who? What's the matter? Where is she?" A chorus of startled questions rose from the boat. Bert said not a word, but sat staring at Mrs. Percival, his face white as the cloth she continued to wave frantically.

"Susie!" screamed aunt Puss. "She's off on a rock, and the tide's almost covered her up. Oh, do hurry!"

CHAPTER VIII.

THE FLOOD TIDE.

AS soon as the White Island party had left that morning, Susie Martin set about her preparations for collecting seaweeds. She borrowed from the camp utensils a two-quart pail, put on her heaviest boots and oldest skirt, and bidding good-by to Mrs. Percival, walked up over the rocks toward the northern side of the island, which was entirely new to her.

The cool air blew upon her cheeks; the gulls could be seen floating silently over the rocks, alighting now and then for a special tidbit, and spreading their soft wings again as an incoming wave almost reached their pretty feet. A song-sparrow chanted over and over his simple refrain, and the sandpipers called anxiously to each other as Susie passed near their four spotted treasures.

Altogether, the world seemed a beautiful place to live in, and Susie's heart was so full of simple content that she sang little snatches of song as she walked.

Before long she paused beside a rose-bush, and gathering half a dozen of the dainty wild blossoms, tucked them into her belt. Susie had not Pet's beauty, nor the sprightliness of the two Percival girls; but no one could have looked at her on this particular morning, as she stood poised on an outcropping ridge of granite, in her sailor suit of dark-blue flannel, the roses in her belt, the sunlight on her hair, and her usually pale, quiet face full of the joy of the morning, without being drawn to this happy young girl, and seeing the lovely soul that looked out of her wide-open brown eyes.

"I guess I'll go over by that pool," she said aloud; then interrupted herself with a little laugh, and a childish jump into the midst of vetchlings and bay. "What fun to talk right out without anybody hearing a word! Miss Martin," she continued, "suppose you and I step down to the water and see if we can find some sea-weeds."

Before she had gone far, she reached the banks of a curious little inlet or basin which was con-

nected with the great ocean outside by only a
narrow strait. It had a floor of silvery sand, and
the water was so clear that every pebble could
be distinctly seen.

Susie was in ecstasies over this pretty sight;
it was like a mermaid's bathing pool. She
resolved to send the boys off on another expedition as soon as possible, while she and the girls,
all of whom had brought bathing-suits, should
float about in its transparent waters, like veritable
sea-maidens.

Leaving this pool with a half-envious glance at
a shoal of tiny fishes that were darting to and
fro in its depths, she turned toward the long,
narrow point of the island, which ran out toward
the north-east, and of which I have already
spoken. Walking soon became harder; and she
had to jump several little chasms, that would
have given her an ugly fall had her foot slipped.
She noticed, as she picked her way carefully
over these rocks, that their surface was studded
with a sort of small dark stone, looking as if
somebody had fired charges of duck-shot into
them. The stones, on closer examination, proved
to be of a deep-red color. She managed to

knock off a fragment of rock containing half a dozen of them, and pocketed it to show Mr. Percival. Nearer the water she crept, until she could reach the exquisite sea-mosses that spread their rare and dainty foliage, and swayed to and fro with every ripple.

"Now, let me see," she said. "I'll begin with the commonest kinds. First, here's this thick, mussed-up rockweed. I suppose I must have a bit of that, though it's clumsy and big."

She pulled off two or three sprays, and was rewarded by finding a more slender and gracefully branched variety clinging to the coarser sort.

From that time, collecting went on rapidly. She made her way out over the slippery, weed-covered rocks, farther and farther from the dry ledges. It was fascinating sport; new varieties, or the hope of them, constantly beckoning her on; and what possibilities of rare species, of the rosy and purple hues she had hung over in the illustrations of her book on seaweeds! Every tuft of rockweed might be hoarding one of these splendid treasures; in each little pool, so invitingly near, there *might* be a rosy mist of

Ceramium or *Callithamnium* awaiting her eager fingers — and the two-quart pail!

A long, squirming frond of kelp drifting by made the girl laugh; for Tom's speculations on the steamer, and the apt comparison made by his father, was known to every one of the party.

"I guess I shall have to leave kelp out of my collection," she soliloquized, as she detached a piece of delicate green dulse from its foothold, and deposited it with the rest.

Had she been less forgetful of every thing but her task, or more used to the sea and its "tricks and its manners," she would have noticed, with a very reasonable apprehension, that the kelp was drifting *in toward the mainland*, and not very slowly, either. From time to time she heard the boom of the surf on the outside of the point, but Mr. Percival's words about the breakers and the flood-tide had entirely passed out of her mind.

"Oh, dear," she exclaimed at length, after a long but successful struggle to gather a fragile mass without tearing it, "I suppose I must go back to camp! All these seaweeds really ought to be arranged before dinner, and " —

She stopped suddenly, just in time to save herself from a wetting, if no worse. As it was, she went in over the tops of her boots before she could check herself at the edge of a rather deep channel between two rocks.

It did not look familiar.

"I must have come another way," she said rather timidly, looking askance at the water sidling to and fro in the little channel.

She clambered with some difficulty around a large slippery bowlder, and would have gone on ; but the moment she reached the other side, she recoiled with a cry of real terror.

Between her and the next large rock, — and that was a long way from firm, dry land, — the water rose and fell, across a space of at least a dozen feet. How deep it was in its shallowest part, she could not tell ; and on either side lay the treacherous depths of the incoming tide. The roar of the surf behind her sounded louder and nearer than before ; in front, the black, silent channel ; the bleached rocks of the island so little way beyond.

And Susie Martin, city-bred girl as she was, could not swim a stroke. To splash about like a light-hearted little mermaid, in a shallow, land-locked pool, was one thing; but to trust herself to those great, silent waves, swinging the sea-weed up and down, to and fro, — she shuddered at the thought.

She realized now that no time was to be lost. Surely, on that bright June day, some help must be near. She climbed to the very highest point of the little promontory left to her, and prepared to wave her handkerchief as a signal.

But to whom should she wave? Her agonized gaze swept the blue, dimpled surface of the ocean. Sails there were in plain sight. But the nearest was miles away. She cried aloud for help. Could Mrs. Percival hear?

"Help! Help! Aunt Eunice! Mrs. Percival! Oh, help!"

Nothing came in answer to her call, — yes, one thing came. Silently, quietly the ocean came, step by step. Closer foamed the white front of the breakers. Deeper, wider, blacker, ran the smooth waters between her and the shore.

Mrs. Percival, for her part, had looked forward to the forenoon as one for "clearing up," and then resting. While she had known considerably less than sixty summers, she was not too young to enjoy a quiet hour or two with nothing to do but to look out upon the broad, sunlit ocean, and look back over her own sunlit life.

Accordingly, when Susie's blue flannel suit had disappeared among the rosebushes, she had set briskly to work, putting things to rights, like the thrifty New-England housekeeper she was. She swept the floor of the cabin (the boys had not thought that necessary), washed out her dishcloths, shook up the bedding, looped back the curtains, brushed up the fireplace, and at last seated herself on the sheltered side of the camp, where she could see the water, and hear its musical fall on the pebbles of the beach a few rods away.

After a while she dozed a little, but awakened with a sudden start, and a feeling that she had heard something unusual.

She listened intently. Solomon had gone in the sloop with the rest; he could not have barked within hearing. Just then a gull uttered a peculiar cry, as it rose from the feeding-grounds on the reef.

Mrs. Percival gave a sigh of relief.

"It must have been that," she said to herself, settling back for another nap. "I, declare I thought"—

She turned pale, and started to her feet. It was *not* the gull, any more than it was Solomon. It was a faint, far-off human cry.

Aunt Puss left behind forty years, at least, as she hurried up the rocks, through the bushes, and across the island.

The cries rang out now, sharp and clear.

"Help! Oh, do come, do come!"

"I'm comin'; I'm comin', dear," screamed aunt Puss, dropping her shawl and her g's in her headlong rush to the rescue.

Down over the ledges, and there she had to stop. Could it be Susie,—that little helpless heap crouching on a black mound of seaweed out there among the breakers? Fifty feet of angry water, no longer black and silent, but hurling itself in solid, roaring masses against the island, and rushing in a great sweep of wave and tide between the girl and the woman.

Aunt Puss wrung her hands in agony. Susie covered her face and was very still. Every few moments a dash of spray flew high over her, drenching her from head to foot. An enormous dark wave came rolling in, its crest curling and rippling, and rearing itself higher and higher.

It broke in a thunderous roar on the outermost reef.

"She's gone; she's gone," moaned aunt Puss.

The water foamed up about the girl until she appeared for a moment actually floating in the sea. Then it receded, and the next wave was not nearly so high.

Susie still clung to the rock; but Mrs. Percival knew the tide was rising, and would ere long roll smoothly half a fathom deep over that last remnant of help or hope. She gave one more look across the water. Susie's head was bent low. She could see that the poor child was praying.

At this moment it occurred to the older woman that she could at least throw out some bits of plank, which Susie might possibly reach when she was finally swept off; though even then she would almost certainly be dashed upon the rocks and lost. It was a faint chance, but the only one. Aunt Puss took it. She turned and ran

away toward the camp as fast as she could,
though it almost broke her heart to do it, as
she saw Susie raise her head, and look after her
beseechingly.

No sooner had she reached the highest point of
the island than she saw, half a mile away, the
sloop foaming through the water towards her.
She shrieked to the people on board, and waved
her apron frantically.

"Oh," she groaned, as Tom waved his hat in
answer, "they think it's only for fun! Oh, if
they should sail by!"

Nearer and nearer, within hearing at last, thank
God!

Then she uttered the cry with which the last
chapter closed.

"*Susie,— she's off on a rock, and the tide's
almost covered her up! Oh, do hurry!*"

By this time the sloop had reached her anchorage, and nearly come to a standstill. Uncle Will
gave his orders sharp and quick.

"Henry, let go that anchor. Randolph, down
with the sail. Let the halyards run. Bert, pull
up the wherry, quick!" He cast off the painter
from the cleat to which it was made fast, as

he spoke. "In with you now; and you, Randolph, take the oars. I'll steer. Now, Eunice, where?"

Mrs. Percival began to explain.

But uncle Will waited for no words. Before she had finished a sentence, the boat was dashing ahead through the channel, toward the open sea.

"Tell me if you see any rocks ahead, Martin," ordered uncle Will. "Pull, Randolph, my boy, every second counts."

The water fairly boiled around the bows of the the boat, urged forward by Randolph's powerful strokes.

"There she is!" cried Bert. "Ah-h, she's gone!"

No, she was not gone; for the wave receding, showed her still clinging desperately to the rock. But she could hardly hold her own against another.

Randolph gave a vicious stroke at the oars. One of them struck a hidden rock which Bert had not seen, in his anxiety to watch his sister.

Snap! and half the oar floated away.

The boat swung round, and rolled helplessly in

the trough of the sea, which now combed and broke in foam on the reefs all about them.

"Give me the other oar, quick!" shouted Mr. Percival, unshipping the rudder and throwing it down, tiller and all, in the bottom of the boat.

Dropping the single oar into the socket made for that purpose in the taffrail, he began to scull with all his might, and to such good purpose that the boat forged ahead swiftly once more.

Susie saw the help close at hand, but she dared not loose her hold for an instant, on the tough rockweed to which she was clinging.

"Now, carefully," called uncle Will, as they drew near. "Jump when I give the word, Susie. Bert will pull you in. *Now,—jump!*"

She turned, and half staggered, half fell into the water just in front of the boat.

Bert, leaning far out beyond the bows, seized her dress, and putting out all his strength dragged her over the rail, coming within an inch of upsetting the whole craft as he did so.

There was no time for words. Mr. Percival backed vigorously. and none too soon. The largest wave they had yet seen towered against the horizon.

It curved and broke with a terrible rush and roar, burying the rock deep out of sight, and hurling the little wherry along on its course at a most unwelcome speed.

Three minutes later they were in smooth water, and in five minutes more aunt Puss had the girl in her arms, pale, trembling, drenched from head to foot, but safe.   -

As the little group stood on the rocks, no one spoke for a moment save Solomon, who did his doggish best to voice the thankfulness of all.

CHAPTER IX.

THE ANCIENT TOWN OF APPLEDORE.

EVERYBODY was so sobered down by Susie's perilous adventure that nothing more was undertaken that afternoon.   Uncle Will vainly tried to divert the minds of the rest with stories and plans for the coming days ; and it was not until the following day that their spirits were fully restored.

Mr. Percival was to leave for Boston by the afternoon boat.   The forenoon was occupied in preparing a grand clam-bake.

A suitable place was found down by the shore ; and Mr. Percival, who superintended the affair, called for flat rocks, with which he began to form a sort of circular bed for the fire.

"Why not build it right on the ledge, father?" asked Tom.   "It's flat there, and would save you all the trouble you're taking."

"Because the heat of the fire goes off too

rapidly into the rest of the ledge, while these small stones hold it. — More rocks, boys."

The little platform was gradually levelled off. Then a fire was kindled, and the young folks despatched to all parts of the island for wood.

Mr. Percival had accompanied the boys in their trip to Appledore that morning, running over with the sloop instead of the row-boat, and had purchased from the hotel a bushel of clams. These were now brought up from the camp and placed near the "bake."

For two hours the fire was kept up. It was a serious expenditure of fuel, Mr. Percival admitted; but it was necessary. "Besides," he said, "the boys could row over to Smutty-Nose any time, and on the eastern end of that island they could pick up a boat-load of drift-wood among the rocks in ten minutes."

At length the rocks were pronounced nearly hot enough.

"Seaweed," called Mr. Percival. "Armfuls of it, boys, — that common rockweed. You can get all you want just below there."

The day was hot, and Tom declared he was going barefoot; a proposition which was viewed

TOM AT WORK.

with marked disapproval by aunt Puss, and bursts of laughter from the girls.

He ran down to the water's edge, and presently returned, loaded with seaweed, and accompanied by Solomon, who frolicked about, expressing his admiration of every thing his master did, and becoming wild with delight when Tom's straw hat blew off, apparently for his especial amusement.

Mr. Percival meanwhile busied himself in breaking off branches of bay, and, using them as a broom, now swept the rocky bed clear from ashes.

"Quick, the clams!" was the next order and willing hands poured them in a heap on the centre of the bed. Seaweed was then piled upon them, and the whole mound began to steam in the most appetizing manner.

"We'll be laying the table," said practical Bess.

"All right, girls. Will you have your dinner here, or in camp?"

"Oh, here, — right on the rocks! That will be lovely."

A table-cloth was brought, out of deference to the earnestly expressed wishes of aunt Puss,

and spread on a flat surface of the ledge that
was sheltered from the direct rays of the sun,
and dishes were arranged upon it. Then Kittie
and Pet gathered wild roses, and decked the
"table" prettily.

Coffee was set a-boiling over a little fire all
by itself; some corn-bread, prepared by Mrs.
Percival's deft hands, was added to the feast;
and now word came from the rocks below, that
"clams were ready."

What fun it was to pull aside the seaweed,
now steamed to a bright grass-green, and dig
out the clams, the rich odor of which made Tom
caper in anticipation (he had found the flinty
ledges rather hard, and resumed his shoes and
stockings), and Solomon turn his head very far
indeed on one side as he surveyed the operation
from a safe distance.

There was a gay frolic over the dinner; nothing
better could have been planned to make all hands
forget the terror of yesterday.

Tom kept bringing aunt Puss more clams and
more clams, until she cried for mercy, and Randolph and Bert took turns in pelting him away
with shells.

"Hullo!" cried the former suddenly. "Has there been a shipwreck, I wonder?"

"What is it, Ran?"

"Why, there's another wherry floating up the channel."

"Let's go for it!" exclaimed Tom. "It will be awfully handy round here. Our boat's too small to hold more than half of us comfortably. Come on, Bert. Don't be greedy. Kit will save two or three clams for you."

The two boys scrambled down over the rocks, pulled up the wherry, jumped in, cast off, and rowed toward the strange little craft that was bobbing about in the mouth of the channel.

"Look out for the rocks," sang out Bert, who was rowing. "There's a tremendous swash here."

They were indeed perilously near the breakers as he spoke.

Tom was now able to lean over and seize the runaway.

"Oars and all in her, Bert," he announced gleefully, "and painter dangling. She must have slipped her moorings. I tell you, it's hard work to keep her off the rocks. Back water, will you, Bert?" he added hastily.

At that moment a loud splash close by attracted their attention.

"I declare," exclaimed Bert, backing water vigorously, "if there isn't Solomon! He thought you were going to leave him, Tom."

"Poor old fellow! I didn't know he could swim a stroke. See him shake his head. I guess he got a mouthful of salt water. Come, boy, come!" And Tom whistled to the dog, who watched him with appealing eyes as he swam after the boats.

By this time Mr. Percival was down on the rocks, ready to help them land.

The dog made the hardest work of all, as he was not used to the water, and did not know how to climb up over the seaweed. Tom had to reach down at last and lift him up bodily by the nape of the neck.

The new boat was carefully examined, but no trace of ownership could be found. The oars were a little lighter and more delicate than their own, as if they were meant for a girl's use. That was all the indication that could be discovered.

It was now time for Mr. Percival to start for Appledore, where he would take the steamer.

"Let's all go over," proposed aunt Eunice,

rather to the surprise of the rest. "We can go in the sail-boat, can't we, William?"

"Certainly," said uncle Will, "lots of room. But how about Susie here? Do you feel equal to it, my girl?"

"Oh, yes!" said Susie, with her gentle smile. "I shall get along nicely. If you want to have any *very* long tramps on the island, I can rest at the hotel."

She was a good deal shaken by her exposure and fright the previous day, as her pale face showed. But a good strong constitution promised to throw off the slight cold and weakness that were the only tangible results from the adventure.

The sail to Appledore was a pleasant one; and Mr. Percival took his departure for Portsmouth .in the steamer, amid a chorus of good-byes and the fluttering of many handkerchiefs. He had promised to return two or three days before the party should break up.

"Now," said uncle Will, "let's visit the old town of Appledore. What do you think, Susie? Can you go with us?"

"How far is it, sir?"

"Just over the brow of the hill, there, beyond the little white summer-house."

"I think I can go, sir. If I'm tired, I can sit down and wait for the rest."

They walked up to the hotel, and along the broad piazza, which led them directly out upon the gray rocks, now almost hidden by wild roses. A path wound up the gentle slope, and they were not long in reaching the little summer-house.

"I think I'll stop here," said Susie; and Mrs. Percival, who was herself still a good deal unnerved, decided to keep her company.

The rest, following uncle Will's lead, scattered over the rocks down the southern slope of the island. Presently their guide halted, pointing to the crumbling rows and angles of walls, that reached nearly to the water's edge.

"Here was the old town two hundred years ago."

"How much of a town was it, uncle?"

"About six hundred people lived here. There was a court-house and quite a noted academy. I'm sorry to say, too, that there were a good many shops where liquor was sold; and I've no doubt it made many a woman's heart ache in these little huts right where we are standing, as it does now in almost every city and town in the land."

"Look!" exclaimed Pet, running on in advance. "I'm sure this was a lane where the girls used to drive the cows home at night."

"And those sumachs," added Randolph, "grew just behind the houses."

"Here's a doorstep where babies sat in the sunshine, and reached out their hands for wild roses."

"Come down here," shouted Tom from a distance. "See what a jolly little cove. The man that lived in that house just above pulled his boat up here when the wind blew foul."

Mr. Percival gathered a few dry sticks, and kindled a fire.

"Not a cone to throw on it," he began with a laugh. But just then Bert Martin appeared with one veritable pine-cone, which he had picked up among the drift-wood in Tom's little cove. It set them all thinking, as they gathered about the fire, of the great, silent forests of Maine, the odorous breath of the pine, the notes of the hermit-thrush at twilight.

"I want Bess to read us a part of Lowell's poem about Appledore," said Mr. Percival, as they threw themselves down on the warm grass, and looked off at the blue ocean. "Here it is, 'Pictures from Appledore.'"

Bess took the little volume which uncle Will had produced from his coat-pocket, and read as follows : —

"How looks Appledore in a storm?
    I have seen it when its crags seemed frantic,
    Butting against the mad Atlantic,
  When surge on surge would heap enorme,
    Cliffs of emerald topped with snow,
    That lifted and lifted, and then let go
  A great white avalanche of thunder,
    A grinding, blinding, deafening ire
  Monadnock might have trembled under;
    And the island, whose rock-roots pierce below
    To where they are warmed with the central fire,
  You could feel its granite fibres racked,
    As it seemed to plunge with a shudder and thrill
    Right at the breast of the swooping hill,
  And to rise again snorting a cataract
  Of rage-froth from every cranny and ledge,
    While the sea drew its breath in hoarse and deep,
  And the next vast breaker curled its edge,
    Gathering itself for a mightier leap.

North, east, and south there are reefs and breakers
    You would never dream of in smooth weather,
That toss and gore the sea for acres,
    Bellowing and gnashing and snarling together;
Look northward, where Duck Island lies,
And over its crown you will see arise
Against a background of slaty skies,
    A row of pillars still and white,
    That glimmer, and then are out of sight.

.   .   .   .

Look southward for White Island Light.
    The lantern stands ninety feet o'er the tide;
There is first a half mile of tumult and fight,
Of dash and roar and tumble and fright,
    And surging bewilderment, wild and wide,
Where the breakers struggle left and right.
    Then a mile or more of rushing sea,
And then the light-house slim and lone;
And whenever the weight of ocean is thrown
Full and fair on White Island Head,
    A great mist-jotun you will see
    Lifting himself up silently
High and huge o'er the light-house top,
With hands of wavering spray outspread,
    Groping after the little tower,
    That seems to shrink and shorten and cower,
Till the monster's arms of a sudden drop,
    And silently and fruitlessly
    He sinks again into the sea.

You, meanwhile, where drenched you stand,
  Awaken once more to the rush and roar;
And on the rock-point tighten your hand,
As you turn and see a valley deep,
  That was not there a moment before,
Suck rattling down between you and a heap
  Of toppling billow, whose instant fall
  Must sink the whole island once for all;
Or watch the silenter, stealthier seas
  Feeling their way to you, more and more;
If they once should clutch you high as the knees,
They would whirl you down like a sprig of kelp,
Beyond all reach of hope or help; —
  And such in a storm is Appledore."

"Oh, it's grand!" exclaimed Pet, as the reader concluded. "I do hope we shall see one hard storm before we go."

"We're pretty likely to. Hardly a fortnight passes without one good blow from the east, even in summer time. Of course in the winter the storms are much wilder."

They wandered about a little after that, picking roses, skipping stones off into the water, and talking quietly.

Tom found himself standing beside his uncle, on the edge of a rocky bluff, at the foot of which the seaweed rose and fell idly. Directly opposite was Star Island, with its hotel and smaller buildings in plain sight. Smutty-Nose was farther to the west, while a mile and a half to the south rose the spire of White Island Light.

"I've been thinking, Tom," said Mr. Percival, laying his hand on the boy's shoulder after a slight pause, "of the little talk you and your father had on the steamer."

Tom gave a careless laugh, and would have turned away.

"I guess it didn't amount to much," he said. "Look at that schooner coming up into the roads, uncle. Do you suppose she is a mackerel fisher?"

But uncle Will was not to be diverted.

"I've been thinking," he repeated more gravely, "how Randolph has set his face steadily to do right, taking the little 'northern cross' for his coat-of-arms. He means to be a lawyer, doesn't he?"

"I believe so."

"Bert Martin has his aim in life; and he is strong, manly, earnest, about it. Look at that weed."

Tom looked. It was not an attractive sight,

that long, flimsy, lazy thing, drifting out to sea with the tide.

"Do you think a boy ought to make up his mind while he's in school, uncle, just what business he'll go into?"

"Not at all, not at all. There are a thousand circumstances which may lead him to change his mind as to the particular calling he will follow. Randolph was telling me the other day, that, until he was thirteen or fourteen years old, he never dreamed of being any thing else than a fireman! Then he wanted to be an artist, and spoiled lots of good paper; then a doctor, and finally a lawyer. I think he'll stick to that." And Mr. Percival gave one of his jolly laughs.

"What difference does it make, then?"

"Just the difference, Tom, between the life of a soldier and a miserable, shiftless creature like the 'poor whites' of the South, during our war, — willing to do a little shooting on the right side, perhaps, if occasion offered; but, on the whole, taking things about as they came, joining neither army, wearing no uniform, anxious only not to have their goods confiscated, and generally to keep out of the way of stray bullets."

Tom flushed, and thought a moment. The kelp still drifted by. In the "roads" between Appledore and Star the schooner he had pointed out rounded gracefully up to her moorings, with sails dropping, and a long seine-boat astern.

"What do you think I ought to do, uncle?"

"Stop floating," said Mr. Percival instantly. "You drift with whatever current happens to take you up, my boy. I saw it that winter when you were at my house, and we had the fires of pine-cones. It was the same in that unhappy affair of Pet's watch and the Indian. As far as I can learn, you have 'drifted' at school, taking only fair rank, when you learn even quicker than your cousin. A good student on the whole, but ready to be carried away by the first scheme that comes up among the boys, and join in mischief without a thought of the consequences."

"How can I stop floating, sir?" Tom asked in low tones.

"Set before yourself a noble ideal of manhood. Resolve to be a good soldier, no matter what position in the army you may fill, or in what regiment you serve. Taking this resolve, follow it firmly. And, first of all, Tom, determine to be

a true, earnest Christian man. Enlist on the
right side, — if you believe that *is* the right side."

"Oh, I do, sir!" exclaimed the boy, startled at
the very thought of being placed outside the faith
he had reverenced, as a matter of course, from
childhood.

"Then," continued Mr. Percival, strongly
moved, "take your stand as a soldier and servant
of Christ. You needn't be afraid of the word
'servant.' St. Paul uses it of himself, and he
was a college graduate and a cultured gentleman."

"What do you think I ought to do first, sir?"

Tom straightened himself up, as if he already
began to feel the honor of his calling.

"Ask the dear Father in heaven to help you,
and show you what to do; to put weapons in
your hands, if only a wooden gun, to drill with;
to make you glad to have Him thinking about you,
as He is this minute. Then do every thing in
earnest, and well. If you play, play with all
your heart and with all your might. If you
study, try to realize that God set that lesson for
you in Virgil, and means you to do your best at
it; if you rest, rest in the best way, and not in

silly excitements that leave you jaded instead of refreshed. Put your heart into every thing your hand finds to do. If you find yourself drifting a foot, drop anchor, moor to something ; or, better still, hoist sail, and shape your course. Never was canvas spread for a noble purpose, my dear boy, that God's wind wasn't filling it before half its folds were shaken out."

Tom turned, and grasped his uncle's hand in both his own.

"I'll try, sir," he said, with a new light in his face. "With His help — and yours — I won't drift another yard."

Mr. Percival held his hands warmly.

"Don't let it make you a particle less merry and light - hearted than before, Tom," he said, as the two walked back toward the rest of the party. "Rather, it ought to make life twice as happy for you, and I believe it will."

CHAPTER X.

A TRUE GHOST STORY.

AT the hotel, to which the whole party now returned, Mr. Percival made inquiries as to the stray wherry. Nothing was known about it there, and the campers concluded to keep it at Duck Island during their stay; at the end of which time they could leave the boat with the Laightons, who promised to do all they could, meanwhile, to find the owner of the little craft.

Without delaying longer, they went on board the sloop once more, and set sail for "home," as they now called Camp Kelp. Tom was unusually thoughtful, but said nothing of his talk with his uncle.

That evening, as they sat around the fire, Kittie read bits from her book about the Shoals, and uncle Will told stories of his adventures at sea during two or three years of sailor life in his boyhood.

"There's one story that I might tell you," said
he, after Kittie had given them a page or two
of history, "if I were not afraid of keeping you
awake to-night."

"Oh, tell it, tell it!"

"I'm so sleepy I can hardly keep awake now-
ow-ow," added Tom, affecting a prodigious yawn,
and indicating to Randolph to follow suit.

"Ah-h-*yum!*" gaped Randolph.

"Hah-yow-yup!" followed Bert.

The girls tried to imitate them, but failed
lamentably, and ended in a shriek of laughter.

"I see you're all dreadfully sleepy," said Mr.
Percival gravely. "So perhaps there isn't much
danger of making you wakeful, after all. But—
Eunice, do you think I'd better tell them? It's
a—Ghost Story!"

The call for the tale was now, of course, louder
than ever, and uncle Will began; first having all
the candles put out, leaving only firelight flickering on the walls.

"The story I'm going to tell you," he began,
"I heard from a grizzled old sailor on the good
ship 'Beacon Light,' which cleared from Liver-
pool one November day in 1844. I was not a

regular sailor, — that is, rated as 'able seaman,'
— but took hold wherever I could, sometimes as
'boy,' sometimes taking my trick at the wheel
in fair weather, and going on the watch regu-
larly with the men. It was about eleven o'clock
at night.

"To pass away the time, we were telling yarns
as sailors do. It was a pitch-black night, with no
moon, and just starlight enough to show you, in
their little needle-points of brightness, how light
it might have been if it were not so fearfully
dark.

"There was an old sailor in my watch whom
everybody called 'Old Bill.' I never knew what
his other name was. Leaning up against the bul-
warks, with no sound in the air but the creaking
of the rigging, and the bubbling of water against
the ship's sides, he told me, in a tone and manner
that it was impossible to disbelieve, this story;
and I will preface it by saying that I myself
believe it to be strictly true."

The girls glanced at each other and drew a little
nearer together. It is one thing to read a story
of this sort in a warm, brilliantly lighted room, or
in broad daylight, and quite another to listen to

the narrator's solemn tones, in a little, wind-beaten hut on a lonely island, in the dark night, by the flashing and dying light of a drift-wood fire.

"A short time before the affair happened, Old Bill said, he had shipped on the bark 'Alba-tross,' then in the spice-trade between the East Indies and New England ports. She was rather a large, awkwardly shaped vessel, with too much beam for her length to cut a graceful figure ; but worse than her ungainly build was the reputation for being 'unlucky.' Now, a sailor's belief in the *luck* of vessels cannot be shaken ; and it really did seem as if some evil fate pursued the dingy 'Albatross.' On her first voyage, the story ran, three men were lost overboard in fair weather, — a huge, solitary wave coming aboard and sweeping them away as if they were chips. A year later she was dismasted in a storm off Cape Hatteras, and was so damaged that her owners thought seriously of breaking her up and selling her for junk. But her hull was found to be sound, so she was re-fitted, and sent out again for further disasters.

"If there was a small hurricane anywhere in the

Atlantic Ocean, she was sure to run into it; a water-spout struck her and carried away two of her boats. They put her in the Gulf trade, and she took small-pox aboard at Key West, and had to be fumigated and quarantined for weeks, while her sister vessels were carrying the most profitable freights of the year. In despair the owners sent the 'Albatross,' which seemed to possess a charmed life, to the Pacific, for a cargo of tea. She rounded the Horn in perfect safety, unloaded cotton goods at Canton, took in her cargo of tea, and was captured by pirates within forty-eight hours after leaving port. The tea-chests were partly battered in, partly thrown overboard, and the bark would have been burned, had not the sudden appearance of an American man-of-war in the offing sent the pirates off in hot haste to their own junk.

"The word got round among sea-going men, as it will, that the mis-shapen 'Albatross' was unlucky; and it was hard work to get able hands to ship in her. The crew was made up at last, as I said, and the vessel, under her shadow of ill-luck, lay in tropical waters at dead of night, in a calm Nearly all sail was set; but they might as well have been stowed in the hold, for all the good they did. The spices on board were loaded in bulk, — that is, not in cases, but just poured in loose, in large compartments of the hold, — and the hot, peppery odor that came up through the hatches, in spite of all the battening, made the air seem more sultry and stifling than ever.

"At a little after midnight there came a cat's paw across the water, just filling out the sails a moment, and causing them to give a listless *flop*, one after another. Pretty soon the water began to roughen up under a squally breeze, that grew stronger every minute. The old 'Albatross' began to bob along through the waves in good style, and the men brightened up ; for although half of them were bound away from home, nothing delights a sailor like a fair wind and a good, lively gait.

"The wind still freshened, not steadily, but in gusts, that took our big fore-and-aft sail out heavily, and brought the lee rail well down. It was a moonless night, like the one on which I heard the story on the 'Beacon Light.' No one of the men, old Bill told me, had noticed that the stars had gone out, one by one.

"A few drops of rain came hissing down. 'We could hear them strike the water,' said Bill, 'though we couldn't see a blink beyond the rail.'

"The captain called the first officer to his side, and presently the latter gave orders to reef topsails. Two men started up nimbly enough, though they hated to take in sail.

"All at once down they came over the main rigging, as fast as they could scramble, before the rest had fairly started up. When they reached the deck, the mate was in front of them.

"'What are you down here for?' said he with an oath. "Lay up there lively. No skulking on the 'Albatross,' I can tell you!"

"To everybody's surprise, the men begged to be let off.

"'What for?' demanded the first officer sternly.

"'There's a strange man up there, sir, already.'

"The mate made them repeat the words, and flew into a rage.

"'Call all hands,' he roared.

"As the men came shuffling aft, muttering against the weather, the 'Albatross,' the owners of her, and every officer on board, a vivid flash of lightning lit up the bark, and every spar and rope of her rigging.

"It was but for a moment ; but every man on deck saw the dark figure resting calmly at the masthead, looking down at them through the blinding lightning and the rain which now fell in sheets.

"'Quartermaster, call the roll,' ordered the captain.

"Every man and boy answered to his name. The voices were all familiar to the quartermaster, and could not have been so counterfeited as to deceive him.

"'Who'll go aloft, and find who that fellow is?' shouted the mate, more in a passion than ever.

"The men hesitated. Sailors are naturally superstitious, and the evil reputation of the 'Albatross' increased their terror. At length two of the oldest and bravest men in the crew — one was the quartermaster himself — volunteered.

They climbed the weather-shrouds, one slightly in advance of the other. Suddenly the quartermaster, who was ahead, gave a shrill cry of fright, and by the lightning, which now blazed out every

few seconds, could be seen swinging himself round
under the rigging, and coming down hand-over-hand
on the back-stay, with his mate hard after him.

"It was several moments before he could speak.
Then he fairly stammered with terror.

"He saw the man or creature plainly, he said,
holding itself by the mast, wagging its head at
him, and rolling a pair of fiery eyes in a manner
dreadful to see. 'Wagging its head, wagging its
head,' the man repeated, in tones scarce above a
whisper, imitating the motion of the apparition.
Nobody could doubt the quartermaster's word.
He was evidently sincere, and thoroughly frightened by what he had seen.

"A loud report, like a gun, and something
white floated away into the darkness. The rain
had beaten the sea down a little, but now it
lessened, and the wind blew harder than ever.

"'There goes the main-tops'l,' said the mate
grimly. 'Just our luck. If the ghost had come
an hour ago, there'd been no harm in it.'

"'Ghost or no ghost, I'll see if it can stand
fire,' cried the captain savagely, hurrying down
into his cabin, and presently returning with a
loaded musket.

"The men were now grouped together around the wheel, — a sad breach of discipline, but who could help it? They wanted to get as far as possible from that terrible mainmast, where they could still see the strange figure wagging its head derisively at them.

"The captain took careful aim, then waited a moment and lowered his gun.

"'Come down out o' that rigging,' he shouted, 'or I'll shoot you where you stand.'

"No movement on the part of the figure, save what seemed a wilder nod of its head.

"The captain took a long, steady aim once more, and, by a brilliant flash of lightning which shone on the pale faces of the men, fired full at the apparition.

"It seemed ages before the next flash. It came. An audible shudder ran through the group of cowering sailors. The strange figure was still there, unhurt, unmoved."

"Did you say you believed this story was *true*, uncle Will?" broke in Bess breathlessly.

"I did, and do. Is anybody sleepy *now?*" he asked mildly.

There was a sound of steady breathing somewhere in the room; but it proved to be only
Solomon, who was dreaming the dreams of a
quiet, respectable dog, undisturbed by phantoms
of any sort.

"Do go on, uncle," said Kittie nervously, putting her arm around Susie, whose great brown
eyes, opened wide, were fixed on the narrator.

"Well, you can guess that nobody went aloft
after that. Nor would the men go below. They
remained on deck, dreading lest each flash of
lightning should reveal the spectre descending
toward them.

"The captain now loaded his gun once more,
ramming down some fragments of a silver half-
dollar. Silver bullets, you know, are supposed
to be fatal to witches and all evil powers.

"Again the summons, the long aim, the flash
of the lightning, and the flash of the musket.

"Again the thick, smothering darkness, the
suspense, the horror at seeing the ghost still
unhurt, with its head wagging more violently
than ever.

"Fortunately the gale abated; and the Albatross held the rest of her canvas, though it must have had a pretty severe strain.

"When the gray dawn broke, the crew, cold, wet, miserable, but gaining courage with the daylight, peered at the mainmast head. Two or three of the men, bolder than the rest, crept forward.

"A shout of derision burst from them. The frightful ghost was " —

The young folks leaned eagerly forward; and Tom even stopped rolling up Solomon's left ear, an occupation in which he had been earnestly engaged for the last five minutes.

"Was nothing more nor less than an old suit of clothes stuffed with straw, and a gourd with eyes, nose, and mouth cut out, tied loosely at the top, so that it 'wagged' at every motion of the vessel."

"But the fiery eyes, uncle?"

"That was the vivid imagination of the already terrified men."

"How came the figure there?"

"The first two men carried it up, it was supposed, and tied it there."

A long sigh of relief and a little laugh followed the end of uncle Will's story.

"Come, boys," said he, rising, "it's time to go to our tent. After all, my ghost story is a good deal like the rest, I expect, if you could only hear the explanation of them."

"Good-night, girls," said the boys in chorus.

"We'll leave you the fire, and take Solomon," added Tom, as he closed the door behind him, and made his way after the others to his bed of straw in the tent.

CHAPTER XI.

LANDING ON MINGO.

RANDOLPH," said Bess, one or two mornings after the ghost story, " I want to row over to Mingo."

" What, that big rock out there? You've seen it half a dozen times, haven't you?"

" Big rock or little island, as you prefer. I haven't seen the top of it yet."

" I don't know how you're going to, unless you engage a balloonist to take you over it on the Fourth of July," laughed her cousin.

" I mean to land on it."

" Land on Mingo! Why, it wouldn't be safe, Bessie. They say no woman ever set foot on that rock. It's just fit for gulls. The sea breaks right over it in storms."

" I want to try it, though. Won't you row over with me, in the wherry, and take a look at it, Randolph?"

"I don't know as I ought to," said the boy
dubiously. "Don't you think we ought to ask
uncle about it first?"

"Oh, he won't care! And, besides, he's off with
Tom and Bert, taking a pull, and won't be back
till noon."

"But they have the wherry."

"We can go in the little castaway. It's just
big enough for two."

Randolph was persuaded, and walked down to
the cove with Bess. Mrs. Percival was taking a
nap in camp, and the other three girls were off
after seaweeds, on the other side of the island.

"There," said Bess, as the boat shot out of the
channel, "isn't this better than doing nothing on
the island?"

Randolph could not but admit that it was. His
long, clean strokes soon drove the boat out of
sight and hearing from the camp, and the two felt
like explorers on new seas.

"Let's go round between the Shag Rocks
first," suggested Bess, "it's so smooth in there."

There were two or three ugly looking reefs to
be avoided; but by rowing slowly, and keeping a
sharp lookout, Randolph brought the boat safely

through the dangerous opening, and they floated quietly on the still water beyond.

"It's just like a lagoon in the Pacific Islands," continued the girl delightedly; "so smooth here, and look, you can see the tops of the breakers over the rocks outside."

"See the fishes." And Randolph pointed down. It was, indeed, a lovely sight. The water was of a clear, translucent green, so faint a hue as to barely pass into the realm of color. The voyagers floated twenty feet above the sea bottom, as if they were poised in the air. Below, long streamers of seaweed waved gently to and fro, or clustered in masses of soft, dull greens and maroons; while among them, feeding, darting back and forth, playing all sorts of pretty antics, swam hosts of small fishes of hues even surpassing those of the mosses. Some of the perch were of rich brown, some of strange copper red, some striped, and others beautifully mottled. Now a brilliant scarlet rock-cod wagged along with pompous mien, while the minnows respectfully made way for their Triton.

The walls of this submarine palace were thickly studded with living stars, and now and then a

ruddy crab sidled along as if intent on catching
some sea-urchin in mischief.

The two spectators in the boat hung over these
wonders as if they feared the gorgeous world
beneath them might vanish at a breath. It
seemed beyond belief that such glories were near
them night and day.

"Well," said Bess at length, with a long sigh
of delight, "I suppose we must move on. I never
did expect to see such lovely things while I lived,
Randolph."

"What do you suppose they are made so beautiful for, away down there out of sight?"

"'He saw that it was good,'" repeated Bess
softly. "Perhaps it was worth while for them to
be made, just for that one minute when He looked .
at them all."

"And what if He looks at them every day!"

"I expect He likes to have every thing *perfect*,
Randolph, don't you?—even the away-down-under-
neath things. Don't you believe He does?"

Randolph nodded in a way that showed he
understood; then gave his whole attention to
extricating the boat from the network of half
hidden rocks into which she had drifted.

Careful manœuvring brought them out again into open water, where the little wherry rose and fell with the long, tireless ground swell.

"Now for Mingo," exclaimed Bess gleefully.

Randolph pulled away lustily, and before long the boat lay in the clear channel between that island and the outer Eastern Rocks, that hem in Shag and Duck Island.

The tide, which was a young flood, was running through this narrow strait so strongly, that Randolph had to keep his oars dipping, like the fins of a fish holding its own against a stream.

"Pretty poor prospect," he remarked, shaking his head, as he viewed the tawny flanks of Mingo.

The island, which is simply a huge, roughly rounded rock rising twenty feet or more sheer out of deep water, towered above their heads. For six to eight feet up, it was clothed in masses of dark rock-weed; above that was the bare, bleached rock, that has weathered the fierce storms of the Atlantic for untold ages.

"I really don't see any place to land," continued Randolph anxiously. "The tide runs like a mill-race here, and you can hear the breakers pounding on the other side."

"Let's try it right where we are — unless you are afraid?"

"Aren't you?"

"Not a single bit."

Randolph would have been more than a human boy, if he could have stood being "stumped" by a girl.

"All right," said he. "If you say so, at it we go. Take the oars, please."

Bess was perfectly at home in a row-boat: so she was not at all surprised or disturbed at his request, with which she complied at once.

Randolph now crept past her to the bow, took the coils of the painter in his left hand, and gave directions.

"You must row straight *at* the rock; not hard, but so as to strike it at exactly right angles. If you find yourself coming up broadside on, back off again with all your might. The sea is rising and falling against those rocks a good three feet, even on this quiet side, and the boat would roll over in an instant."

Bess began to repent of her determination, and even faltered out a word or two as to giving it up; but Randolph was busy giving orders, and didn't hear her.

"Steady, steady; the minute I reach the rocks, push off again. I'll keep hold of the painter."

Bess pulled a slow stroke, straight toward the rock; but, as she drew near, the strong tide swept the stern round, in spite of her utmost efforts.

"Back, back!" cried Randolph, seeing the danger.

Three times they tried it, and each time backed away hastily to avoid being swung against the rocks broadside on, and rolling over.

As they neared it the fourth time, Randolph gathered himself, and quick as a flash leaped ashore, holding on with his hands and feet like a cat. He held tightly to the end of the painter, which had been lengthened to keep the boat out at her moorings near the camp.

Bess backed water a few strokes.

"Now turn round," shouted Randolph, "and face the bows. Take in your oars when I give the word, and I'll haul the boat up. Be ready to jump. I'll help you get ashore."

The programme was carried out to a nicety. Up came the wherry; Randolph leaned out over the water, and holding the nose of the boat a mo-

ment against the seaweed, grasped Bessie's hand.
One good pull and a jump, and with beating heart
the girl scrambled up to a safe niche, while her
cousin took a turn with the painter around a point
of rock.

"It may capsize," he panted, as he joined Bess.
"But we can easily right it if it does."

They climbed side by side to the very summit
of Mingo, and stood there with glowing cheeks
and dancin' eyes. It was a great feat to have
landed on that desolate rock, they knew ; but even
then they did not realize how they had taken their
lives in their hands in the midst of those reefs,
the swell, and the swift, treacherous tide.

"I suppose we needn't hurry to return," said
Randolph, picking out a comfortable seat, and
. wiping his forehead. "Uncle won't be back for
at least two hours."

"D you know what this makes me think of,
Ran ?"

"Robinson Crusoe?"

"Not exactly. It seems as if there had been a
great flood, and we had taken refuge on the very
last, highest mountain-peak, with all the rest of
the world under water."

"There's something like that in Ovid, — Deuca-
lion and Pyrrha, you know. They found themselves left this way; and Jupiter, I believe it was,
told them to pick up rocks and throw them behind
them. As fast as they did so, the stones turned
into men and women."

"Must have been a hard-hearted set!"

"I wonder if any Indians ever climbed up on
this rock."

"Shouldn't be surprised. There's a story about
their going out to Star Island, I believe, and cap-
turing everybody except Betty Moody. There's
a cave there now, the book says, where she is
supposed to have hidden. Do you remember
that hard feeling you used to have against
Herbert?" asked Bess, after a pause.

"I guess I do. Queer, isn't it, what good
friends we are now? I hate to think how I felt
about him sometimes last winter."

"He's a splendid fellow, Randolph. But I shall
always be glad you made the first move toward
friendship."

They talked on carelessly, enjoying to the full
the beauty of sky and sea.

"What a funny cloud that is!" said Bess presently, pointing toward the north-east.

Randolph was just then lying on his back, and watching the slow, graceful movements of a gull, who was sweeping to and fro above them, praying with all her might for her daily bread, and doing her best to answer her own prayer.

"All clouds are funny," remarked Randolph sententiously, without stirring. "I see one now, that looks exactly like a pig, with a crocodile chasing it. My, what a mouth!"

"No, but there's something queer about this one," persisted his companion. "I wish you'd leave your pig a minute, and look."

He raised himself lazily on one elbow, and looked in the direction indicated.

"Humph! 'Tis odd, isn't it? Looks like a thick white blanket. And it isn't moving a bit."

"Yes, it is, too. It's twice as thick as when I first saw it, and I'm sure it's coming this way very fast."

"I know," said Randolph suddenly. "It's fog, —a regular bank. There it goes now, right over a schooner. It can't be more than three or four miles away."

They got interested in watching the approach of the lengthening and deepening fog-cloud.

"Of course it can't bother us any," said Randolph, seeing that Bess was getting a little uneasy. "We're so near camp that we could find our way there with our eyes shut."

"There's another boat drifting about," exclaimed Bess, shortly afterward. "I never saw so many stray boats."

Randolph looked at the little craft, courtesying up and down on the waves as it was swept off toward the mainland. His glance was first careless, then interested, then alarmed. With a pale face he sprang to his feet and hurried to the edge of the rocks, from which he could see the point where he had landed.

"What is it? What has happened?" cried Bess, frightened at the look in his face.

"That was *our* boat you saw drifting away. She's got free, somehow, chafing and pulling against the rocks. And now — look at her!"

They could just see the little speck rising and falling in the distance. Even as they looked, the wherry was tossed up on a wave, which broke over a hidden rock, and rolled completely over.

At the same time, the boat, the distant reefs, gulls, rocks, islands, except the one under their

feet, faded from view as if by magic.   They could
hear the breakers on all sides, but could only see
a dull gray expanse of mist blending with the gray
water.

The fog bank had reached Mingo.

CHAPTER XII.

OFF CEDAR LEDGE.

WHEN Mr. Percival started out that morning with Bert and Tom, he told them that he wanted to see how well they could pull together. He would act as coxswain, he said, and he proposed to give his crew a little training. There was a spare pair of oars kept in the sloop, in case of emergency, and these were now brought into requisition.

Bert proposed that they should use the idle pair in the castaway (that is what they all called the little wherry that they had picked up), but they were found to be too light to match the regular working oars of the larger boat.

"Which way are you going, uncle?" asked Tom, who pulled stroke.

"Well, I think we'll head due south, first. That will just carry us by the end of Appledore. I wish we had a compass on board ; then we could do some really scientific navigation."

The boys pulled away lustily, and in ten minutes they were abreast the red summer-house on the outer bluffs of Appledore. Some ladies who were grouped upon the rocks below waved their handkerchiefs; and Mr. Percival, as captain of his vessel, responded gallantly by raising his hat.

"If we had Ran with us, we'd give 'em the Harvard cheer," observed Tom, bending to his oars. "Where away, now, uncle Will?"

"Steady, as she goes, my lad, until we're well out of line with the reef that makes out from the south-east side of the island.

"There's where a vessel is supposed to have gone ashore," he added, "loaded with treasure. I never walk past the place without looking down, half-expecting to see an old Spanish dollar shining among the rocks."

He now brought the boat's head round to the west, and they passed midway between Appledore and Malaga, which is connected by a breakwater with Smutty-Nose.

"What's that between the big island and the little one?" inquired Bert. "Looks like a fort."

"That is Haley's sea-wall. Samuel Haley used to own Smutty-Nose, and lived in that low, gray house just beyond the wharf. Suppose we run up into the cove and see the old place?"

The boys were rather glad to rest their arms, and, mooring their boat to a rude ladder which was nailed against the wharf, scrambled up, followed by Mr. Percival.

The whole place was redolent of fish ; for this is the only island of the group that still supports a seafaring population (of a dozen or so). The fish that are cured on Smutty-Nose are to this day noted for their fine flavor.

After a hasty glance at the flakes and storehouse, Mr. Percival led the boys up the little rocky path between the houses. He pointed out a small garden, surrounded by a curved stone wall like the stern of a ship. All the rocks, big and little, were flecked with golden lichen.

" Haley was the life of the place," said uncle Will, as they paused beside the gray old building which was once his home. " You can find out all about him in Mrs. Thaxter's book. He made the sea-wall that we noticed connecting this island with little Malaga, put up salt-works, built a ropewalk nearly three hundred feet long, erected windmills, and planted an orchard, all on this small island.   But what I like best to remember of his rugged, independent life is, that every evening he placed in that window, — it was his bedroom — a candle that burned all night.   The sailors in these waters must all have known the old man's light, and blessed his loving thought of them, on many a stormy night, as they caught sight of the tiny spark."

"How long ago was this, uncle?"

"He died sometime between 1810 and 1820. The Spanish ship 'Sagunto,' Mrs. Thaxter tells us, was wrecked on this island in 1813, on a bitterly cold winter's night.   A part of the crew were drowned, and a part cast ashore still living. Those who had strength crawled toward Haley's light.   Two of them got as far as the stone wall in front of his house, but could go no farther, and perished there.   Every soul on board, says the story, was lost.   That we know was false, thank God!" said uncle Will fervently.

"Did any escape, then?"

"Every*body* on board was lost, my boy.   The souls that had worn them for a little while lived on ; or rather, I think, began to really live for the first time.   Poor old garments!   They were found

all along the shore, and buried — fourteen of
them — in that little field."

They walked on a few steps, through red and
white clover blossoms and lush grass, to the row
of little headstones, and, as they looked at them,
thought of the grand music of the stormy ocean,
with which those fourteen Spaniards walked from
this world to the next, where there is no more sea.

"Here is the story of Samuel Haley, cut in
stone," said Mr. Percival, taking them a little
farther on. "The date of his death should probably be a little later; else the Gosport records of
the wreck of the 'Sagunto' are wrong."

The boys read : —

"In memory of Mr. Samuel Haley

Who died in the year 1811

Aged 84

He was a man of great Ingenuity

Industry Honor and Honesty, true to his

Country & A man who did A great

Publik good in Building A

Dock & Receiving into his

. Enclosure many a poor

Distressed Seaman & Fisherman

In distress of Weather "

The boys walked about the old buildings a little longer, glad to have seen one island "of Shoals" which has remained almost unchanged from its ancient estate.

There was a large boarding-house, or inn, near the breakwater, and here they were served with lemonade by a kindly lady with snow-white curls.

But Tom's spirits could not long be quieted by the shadows of the Past. He was emphatically a boy of the Present. He had seen enough of Smutty-Nose, and was getting hungry.

"About time to go aboard?" he suggested.

Mr. Percival "was willin';" and the three walked down to the landing, clambered to their boat, and were soon shooting over the water once more.

"I did mean to go round outside of Star," said uncle Will, looking at his watch. "But it's getting so late that perhaps we'd better pull right out between Star and Cedar, and then bear up to the north again, toward home."

There was quite a sea running through this narrow passage, and the boat rose and fell in a way that made rowing a difficult matter to boys who were used only to smooth water.

Before long, Tom caught a good-sized "crab,"

and went heels-over-head backward into Bert's lap.

"Tom," remarked Martin gravely, as that young man resumed his thwart, and made a wild double stroke at nothing, the boat tossing up at that moment, "please to recollect that this is not a flying-machine, — nor a diving-bell," he added, as a roller came along, and the stroke plunged both oars in up to their leathers.

"All very well for you," panted Tom, "looking at me, and seeing all my mistakes, so you needn't follow suit. I don't believe you've pulled an ounce for the last half mile."

Mr. Percival did not laugh at the boys' fun. He was steering mechanically, but at the same time was looking intently ahead, and to the right.

"What is it, uncle?" asked Tom, observing his silence. "A whale — or another floating text for me?"

Mr. Percival seemed hardly to hear his question.

"Boys," said he, after a minute, "I don't like the looks of that fog bank outside. If you can pull a little harder without hurting yourselves, I wish you would do so. Let me change places with one of you."

But neither one of the rowers would listen to this; and, indeed, the older man was needed at the tiller, to keep the boat up to the sea that now began to roll in from the east before a freshening breeze.

They pulled lustily, but before they were past the outer end of Smutty-Nose, the fog was upon them. The change from a summer sea, with islands, houses, and vessels in plain sight, to gray, desolate mid-ocean, was marvellous.

"Whew!" whistled Tom, "didn't that drop quick? It's so thick we'll row right up into it, if we don't look out."

"Keep up a good stroke, boys. The quicker we get back to camp now, the better. I hope all the rest are ashore."

They pulled in silence for ten minutes. The sea was no rougher, and the wind seemed to die down with the arrival of the fog; but the swell was so heavy that the steersman had continually to head up into it, to escape the danger of an overturn in the trough.

"We must be well alongside Appledore," said he at length.

"If we are," remarked Bert, "I don't see why

we don't hear the surf. Don't you remember how loud it was as we went by this morning?"

There was enough force in the boy's reasoning to make Mr. Percival uneasy.

"I'd give a good deal for a compass just now," said he. "I can tell about how the boat *heads*, by the direction of the waves; but what our real course is, I can't tell. There's one force at work that baffles me."

"What is that, sir?" inquired Tom with a touch of anxiety in his voice.

"The tide."

"The tide! Why, you know whether it's ebb or flood, uncle?"

"Yes. But among these islands none but the old shoalers are acquainted with the various currents and sweeps it makes. It may now be setting us north toward home, or directly south, or right toward Appledore."

The stillness of the fog was more oppressive than can be imagined by any one who has not been similarly overtaken. Only a few minutes before, the air had been full of sunlight and white-winged birds, sails had gleamed here and there, children could be seen on the rocks at Appledore, and smoke curling up from the Star Island houses. Now every sound seemed muffled. They could not even hear the breakers. In this way they rowed in silence for fifteen minutes more, straining every nerve to catch the slightest noise, beyond the regular plash of the oars, and the little chop that had come in with the east wind, against the bows of the boat.

"We can't be far from Duck Island, at any rate," began Mr. Percival. "If we hadn't"—

He stopped suddenly, for a strange thing happened. The sea had not been running high; indeed, it would have been nearly smooth, but for the long swell, and slight easterly ruffle. But, as Mr. Percival was speaking, the water in front of the boat, not fifty yards away, rose as if a giant were coming up from the ocean depths. A huge, dark mound of water, curling a moment, then breaking in a roar of foam, whitening the sea in all directions, and boiling like a cauldron around the wherry, which was tossed like a chip on the receding wave, — that was what they saw.

Even as the sound of the breaker died away in long, melancholy moan, another rose behind it, blacker, more huge and threatening, than the first.

"Back water, back water, for your lives!"
cried uncle Will, his face blanched at the sight.

The boys needed no urging. Fortunately
neither of them missed a stroke, and the wherry
darted backward from the swiftly advancing wave,
which reared itself high into the fog, and thun-
dered down after them.

The boat nearly capsized when the heavy ripple
from the breaker struck it; but Mr. Percival's
hand was steady, and only a gallon or two of
water dashed in over the gunwale.

"What was it?" gasped Tom and Bert, as soon
as they were out of the reach of these monsters.
Uncle Will shook his head.

"I can't tell you, my boys. It seems to me it
must be one of the outlying reefs of Duck Island.
But, no, for if it was, we could hear the breakers all round us. It is some lonely rock, away
from the main group, that's sure."

The boys' hearts thumped. Not know where
they were! Who could tell, then, in that stifling,
deathlike fog, whether the next rock might not be
just in front of them, or on either side? Where
should they go? Which way could they turn?

"The rock was hardly above water," added

uncle Will, who had been thinking with all his might. "Just before the second wave rolled up, I could see over and beyond the reef, altogether. There is just one rock about here that answers the description," he continued slowly.

The boys waited, only rowing enough to keep steerage way on the boat.

"That is Cedar Ledge."

"Cedar Ledge! I thought that was south-east of Star Island," exclaimed Bert.

"So it is. And if I am right the tide has swept us out of our course, as I feared. In that case, we are nearly three miles from camp."

"And drifting still farther away!"

"And drifting still farther away."

"Let's pull, then, so as not to lose any more ground."

Tom gripped his oars, and prepared to put in all his strength.

But his uncle asked quietly, "In which direction, Tom?"

The boys looked at each other, at the calm, strong face before them, at the fog, and the gray waves. Which way! It was true; not one on board had the slightest idea in which direction home lay. They were as fairly lost as if they were in mid-Atlantic, a thousand miles from land. That moment, for all they knew, they might be driving directly upon a hidden reef.

To add to their distress, they began to be extremely thirsty. They glanced nervously over their shoulders at every splash of a wave, half expecting to see another huge breaker threatening them. Mr. Percival observed their startled looks, and spoke quietly, —

"Tom — Bert — I'd rather be here, in the hollow of His hand, than anywhere in the universe empty of Him. Now let us help Him to help us out of our danger. Ready, pull!"

There was something in this man's cheery, confident tones that brought the blood back to their checks, and hope to their hearts. They bent to their oars with a will, and, as the boat darted ahead again, felt the relief of actually doing something.

An hour passed. Rain had now begun to fall; at first in a light drizzle, then in a downright pour. Uncomfortable though this was, Mr. Percival took it for a hopeful sign, that the fog would not last long. He looked at his watch. It was a few minutes after two.

The boys rowed slowly, and sucked the drenched sleeves of their jackets, which gave them some relief from their thirst.

They had stopped for a moment to listen for breakers, when Bert declared he heard a sound like rushing water. The rest had hardly time to look in the direction he indicated, when a white cloud seemed suddenly to grow out of the sky, and hang almost above them, growing larger every instant. A moment later all three discovered its true character, and sent up a wild cry.

The big, three-masted schooner — for such it was — swept up toward them, replying to their shout with a dismal note from a fog-horn.

The boys pulled for dear life, as they had from Cedar Ledge, and managed to get out of her path. At the same time, Mr. Percival shouted to the lookout, "A rope! Throw us a rope!"

He had uttered the words on the spur of the moment, with hardly a thought.

The sailor, however, catching the meaning of the shout, and taking in the situation at a glance, sprang to a coil of rope that hung over a pin just inside the rail of the schooner, and flung it toward the wherry. Bert caught it, and perhaps would

have held on tight and let his boat be dragged
under, had not the sailor shouted, " Pay out ! Pay
out ! "

He did as he was bidden, and so relieved the
strain a little. He was now crouching in the bows
of the boat, around which the water bubbled
merrily as she was towed along.

Meanwhile, the skipper of the vessel gave one
or two sharp orders, and she luffed up just
enough to shake her large sails and so materially
slacken her speed. She had not been going very
fast, as the east wind had nearly died away, and
was now beginning to come in little puffs from
nearer the north. Her true course was a little
north of north-west.

Two minutes later the boat was drawn up alongside the schooner, and the three campers climbed
aboard. Before Mr. Percival had fairly gained
the deck, the schooner had filled away again,
and stood on her course with the wherry in tow.

The skipper was a bluff, red-faced, good-natured
man, every inch a sailor.

" All adrift ? " he asked, as his three unexpected
passengers made their way aft. " Where d'ye put
out from ? "

Mr. Percival explained their trip, and asked in his turn, "Where is the 'Nancy Lee' bound?"

"To Porchm'uth," answered the captain. "But it's one thing to be bound, and another thing to be thar," he added, as the lookout in the bows, hardly distinguishable through the dense fog, gave a long blast from the horn, lingering gloomily on the final note.

"Do you mean that you are in doubt as to reaching Portsmouth to-night, sir?" inquired Mr. Percival in some anxiety.

"No doubt at all!"

"Oh, excuse me!" said Mr. Percival. "I thought you said" —

"I says exactly what I means; and that is, thar's no doubt in the matter. I don't go up the river to-night for nobody in this thick weather. We've got to anchor somewhere's down near Whale's Back, that's sure."

"How far are we from the Shoals now?"

"Oh, Hog Island" (the coasters do not take kindly to the new name "Appledore") "is about five mile from here, nor'no'th-east! I give her a good berth, I can tell ye."

"You can't be far from Whale's Back Light, then?"

"Reach it in less'n fifteen minutes. Hark, hear the whistle?"

The steam-fog whistle on the light-house sounded plainly, and presently they passed the bell-buoy, tolling dismally.

A little farther, and the sails came creaking down, the anchor-chain rattled out from the bows, and the "Nancy Lee," with a fog-horn calling at intervals for everybody to steer clear, swung at her moorings, waiting for the storm to clear away. The rain ceased falling before five o'clock, but the fog seemed thicker than ever. It was plain that no one on board would reach Portsmouth that night.

CHAPTER XIII.

THE CASTAWAYS.

RANDOLPH and Bess looked at each other in blank dismay.

"What's to be done, Ran?" inquired the girl, in a voice that tried to be brave.

Randolph shook his head.

"I don't see how we are to get away from here, Bess, until the fog lifts."

"Don't you believe uncle Will will come off after us?"

"In the first place, I'm not sure that he can get back to camp himself in this thick weather. If he did, nobody knows where we have gone. You know we went off without telling a soul. Aunt Puss was asleep, and the girls were away."

Bess looked sober.

"And besides," concluded Randolph, "if uncle got home, and knew we were on Mingo this minute, it would be as much as his life was worth to try to row here among all the reefs, with the fog so thick he could hardly see a boat's-length ahead."

"Can't we shout?"

"No use. Wind's the wrong way. If the girls should happen to catch the sound, it would only frighten them half to death."

"I *don't* see what we're to do, then," exclaimed Bess, looking vainly off through the mists, in the direction taken by the runaway boat.

"Well, Bess, I wouldn't have talked things right out so plain, if you had been a scarey sort of a girl. Not that there's any great danger, though. Only we're liable to be pretty uncomfortable before we leave this rock."

"What time is it, Ran?"

Randolph consulted his watch.

"It's just five minutes before twelve. Suppose we explore our desert island."

They walked carefully along the ledges, peering into all the crevices, and taking note of the general features of the lonely rock. Randolph gave a shout as his eye caught a bunch of driftwood in a narrow cleft.

"Just what we want!" he exclaimed, hurrying

down to gather it up, and carry it out of reach of
the tide.

As the island was something less than a hundred
feet long, it didn't take a great while to finish the
tour of exploration.

All the wood they found, they brought carefully
to a place near the summit of Mingo, where a
projecting rock would partly shelter it from the
damp. When the last block and splint were laid
on the pile, they found they had quite a stock of
fuel ; enough to keep a fire going several hours,
should they need it, Randolph said.

Near the "wood-box" there was a depression
in the ledge, with a wall of rock toward the north
and east, and a floor sloping slightly outward
toward the sea. This spot they decided to make
headquarters during their enforced stay on
Mingo.

"Now, Bess, let us take an inventory of the
larder."

"The larder ! Why, there isn't a thing to eat,
except rocks and seaweed."

"My dear little cousin, did you ever know an
old camper to start off on an expedition without
something eatable in his pocket ? Look here !"

Randolph pulled out four good-sized pieces of pilot-bread from his jacket pockets, and laid them triumphantly on the ledge before her.

Bess smiled faintly. "They're good while they last, Randolph, though they don't look exactly juicy. But suppose we have to stay here 'way into the afternoon?"

"Afternoon! Bess," said Randolph earnestly, "we might just as well look things in the face. I haven't the least idea of getting away from here before to-morrow morning."

The girl was silent for a moment. In that pause she could hear the waves breaking dully against the outer end of the island, as the tide crept up. Somehow the place seemed terrible to her, with its bleached ledges, its utter loneliness, and its memories of wreck and death.

But Bessie's training stood her in good stead. If in her inmost heart she wanted to break down and have a good cry, she stifled the impulse, and remembered, hard, that she and her cousin, as well as those left in camp, were in safe keeping; and neither sea nor storm could harm them against their Master's will.

She looked up brightly, and said, "We're on a

good, solid rock, anyway, Ran. How thankful I am that we're not in that little boat out there in the fog, tossing about among those reefs!"

"Aren't you afraid?"

"A very little bit, perhaps," she answered candidly. "But even that bit is going away, I think. It doesn't seem half so bad as when you first spoke."

"That sounds like 'Captain Bess,'" said Randolph with a relieved laugh. "Now that we've looked on the worst side, I'll tell you what I've concluded to get for dinner."

Bessie glanced at the dry fragments of biscuit.

"No, I mean besides that; though, I tell you, there's worse food in the world than pilot-bread! You just now said there was nothing on the island but rocks and seaweed. You left out our livestock."

"What do you mean, Ran? Surely you wouldn't harm a gull?"

"Not a bit of it — yet — supposing there was any way to get one, which there isn't. I'll show you. Look!"

He sprang down to the water's edge, stooped over a little rift, lifted some of the long streamers of seaweed, and re-appeared with a double-handful of large black mussels and snails.

Bess eyed them rather doubtfully.

"Don't you see?" continued the boy enthusiastically. "The snails make the very best kind of bait, and they're sweet as chestnuts to eat. We'll have perch for dinner, and baked shell-fish for supper."

"But how are you going to get your fish?" laughed Bess, growing interested.

For reply, her companion pulled out a roll of perch-line. "Always have a fish-line," he explained. "I've got caught away from camp, up in the Maine woods, when it came in handy, I can tell you."

"I suppose we shall miss salt at our meals," said Bess, "but we can easily do without."

Randolph's eye roamed along the roughened, irregular surface of the rock.

"Wait a bit."

He left her once more, and presently she saw him pinching something up in his thumb and finger, and running back to her.

"Try that, fellow-traveller."

She tasted the grayish powder daintily.

"Randolph, — it's salt! Did you ever!"

"Never!" replied Randolph gleefully. "But
I noticed that salty crust in two or three places,
when we first came up. There was more of it
on Shag than there is here. Let's gather some,
and save it up in a dry place. It looks more like
rain every minute."

"I suppose the waves dash up on the rocks,
and the water evaporates," said Bess, scraping
busily.

"That's it. You heard uncle Will tell how
the sea runs here, in a storm."

"Just think, Ran, of some great wave coming
across the ocean, and finally crashing up onto
this lonely rock, just to bring us a little salt!"

It was, indeed, a wonderful way of answering
a prayer for "daily bread." What a messenger
to send with it, to His children!

They both thought of it reverently as they rose
from their task, and watched the breakers rolling in through the fog, and throwing themselves
at their feet.

"Now, Bess," said Randolph, "we'll— But
what's the matter?"

Something in her face had stopped him.

"I just happened to think, — I don't know that I ought to speak of it, but it came to me all at once, — what are we to do for water? I'm beginning to be dreadfully thirsty already."

Randolph was staggered a minute. He had not thought of that, and the very suggestion instantly roused his own thirst.

"I don't know," he said slowly: "it seems as if there must be some way, with fire, and all this water around us."

"I read somewhere," volunteered Bess, "that one could dip his handkerchief in salt water, and wring it out; then dry the handkerchief, dip and wring out again; and so on, till the salt would be taken all out it, and shaken off, dry, from the cloth."

"I've tried that," said Randolph; "and, to tell the truth, Bess, it didn't work worth a cent. I might have been patient and tried longer, I suppose; and, if it comes to the worst, I'll sit here and wring all night."

"Couldn't we" —

But what Bessie's plan was, Randolph never asked. As if in direct answer to their longings, a drop of water struck against the girl's face.

"It's raining! Plenty of fresh water now, Bess."

"How shall we catch it?"

They tried in vain to improvise some sort of a bag or basin with hats and sacks. But they might have been spared their trouble.

"Look!" exclaimed Randolph. "Mingo will catch the rain and save it for us!"

It was true. Here and there, all over the little island, were hollows in the rock, where even now the rain began to collect in tiny pools, crystal clear. As it was now pouring hard, they jumped down into their shelter, where the rock had just overhung enough to keep off most of the rain.

There they sat for two long hours, watching the gradual approach of the tide, the white rush of the waves, and the myriad hissing rain-drops on the heaving surface of the gray ocean.

During a slackening of the shower, they dodged out and drank a long draught from one of the little rocky reservoirs. The water was slightly brackish from the previous baths of salt waves; but on the whole it was drinkable, and refreshed them greatly.

"It's lucky we got that wood up," said Randolph, as they crept back to their shelter. "We'll have a good fire by and by, rain or no rain."

By the middle of the afternoon they were pretty well chilled, although — thanks to the overhanging rock — they were only wet in "local areas," as Randolph expressed it.

The rain now ceased falling, and the fog hung round the islands thicker than ever.

"Seems to me the wind's getting round to the north," remarked the boy, crawling out and stretching his cramped limbs. "What did you do with the salt, Bess?"

"Put it in the envelope of that letter I received yesterday, and tucked it way inside my dress. It's all nice and dry."

"Good! Here goes for some dinner. I'm hungry's a bear. Hullo, there's some more wood!"

He managed to secure two or three large pieces of joist that were drifting in with the tide, and had lodged against the rocks. Of course they were dripping wet, but would do very well for a backing to the fire.

Bess helped as well as she could, getting snails

and mussels, at Randolph's suggestion, until a
good store was laid by. The fish-line was un-
rolled, the hook carefully baited, and cast out into
the channel. It had hardly disappeared below the
surface when there was a tug. Randolph pulled
in excitedly, and brought a big perch to the very
rock where he stood, when the fish gave a sudden
flop and was off.

"Give us another bait, Bess!" he shouted.
"There's provision enough here for an army."

The next cast was more successful : it brought
in a good-sized perch, not quite so big as the first.
Another and another followed, until half a dozen
were flopping about over the rocks.

" Haven't you about enough, Ran?" called out
his comrade. "Poor little things, I wish you'd
put them out of their misery."

" They don't feel it," said Randolph, keeping
his eye on his line. "The oxygen is just like
laughing-gas to 'em. I want to get one more.
Gracious! what's got hold now?"

He pulled away, till a big red snout came above
water.

"It's a rock cod!" he called out excitedly.
" Look at him, Bess, — a perfect whale!"

It took some really scientific "playing" to get the great fellow ashore.

"Four pounds, if he's an ounce," said the fisherman with exultation. "Hasn't he a splendid color?"

But Bess was too tender-hearted to watch the fish; and Randolph, taking them to the other side of Mingo, killed and dressed them alone.

"Where shall we have the fire, Ran?"

Bess had busied herself in whittling kindlings, picking out suitable blocks of wood.

"Right here in this little corner, in front of our shelter; then we shall get the benefit of the heat. Got some splendid kindling, haven't you?"

"Here's that letter that came yesterday. I hate to burn it, but we'd better make sure of our fire. How many matches are there?"

"If we were on a desert island in a book, Bess, there'd only be a match and a half; and the whole one would go out, with intense excitement over the other" —

"Which would 'sputter feebly' and burn at last. I know. Well?"

"Look at that, cousin mine!"

He showed a well-stocked match-box. "We

aren't reduced to rubbing two sticks together yet," he laughed.

It was a point of honor in the Percival family, to have the fire lighted with the first match. To have recourse to a second, was a matter of reproach; the unfortunate boy or girl who only succeeded with a third was openly derided; while only pity was reserved for attempts beyond that number.

Randolph's first match caught nicely, and the delicate Boston stationery blazed up; then came Bessie's shavings, small splints of wood, and lastly good-sized blocks.

The moment the flames mounted merrily into the foggy atmosphere, the whole character of the place changed. It was no longer a desolate, storm-swept, wave-washed ledge, fit only for wild fowl to scream over, or the treacherous tides to creep about, lifting its black seaweeds; but a home, with a hearthstone, and a warm, living heart. Surely, of all the material gifts God has given to His children, none is more precious than that strange, beautiful creature we call Fire.

The two castaways felt the influence of it, and brightened at once.

ON MINGO ROCK.

"Name it, Bess," said Randolph, stretching
out his hands to the genial blaze, and feeling the
comfort of it flood his whole being. Who can
wonder that in olden times men have considered
fire the most direct means of communicating with
God,—kindling it upon altars, keeping it alight
in sanctuaries, sending up prayers in smoking
incense, even worshipping the fire itself, as a
type of Him who is all powerful, all beautiful,
and all helpful?

"Camp Trust," said Bess simply.

Randolph understood, and bared his head a
moment. It was with no grave faces, however, that they began the preparation of their
meal.

There were no loose rocks whatever on Mingo.
The only way, therefore, to cook the fish, was to
roast them on a spit. With one perch "sizzling"
on each side of the fire, the cooks had a merry
time of it.

The fish were done at last; at least, the chief
cook pronounced them so. They were undeniably
smoky, and one of the best pieces had tumbled
off into the ashes, from which it was rescued in
rather a demoralized condition; but, with the aid

of a little salt, — "from our own farm too," remarked Randolph, — it had a delicious flavor.

Bess leaned back against the rock, munching
contentedly at her biscuit and fish.

"Really, Ran," said she, "if it weren't for the
folks being frightened about us, I should say this
was the very jolliest afternoon yet."

"Man," said Randolph gravely, "is said to be
the cooking animal. I regret, Miss Percival, that
you should think so much of creature comfort."

"I wish you'd pass me some water, Randolph."

"Awfully sorry, but the goblet's too heavy."

Bessie scrambled up with a laugh, and, kneeling
at the nearest pool of rain-water, drank her fill.

When dinner was over, they found to their
surprise that it was five o'clock. Half the biscuit
was saved for the next meal. Randolph resumed
his fishing, and added a dozen more perch to his
stock of provisions. In taking in the last one, he
met with a bad accident. The hook caught in the
rocks far below low-water mark; and when he
pulled up the line there was neither fish nor hook
there, only the shank of the latter, showing how
it had broken.

"Never mind," said he, noticing his companion's

concern. "I've got enough for breakfast; and, if we need more, I can rig a bent pin so as to catch a clumsy fish like a perch."

It grew dark, and the sea grew more mysterious in its moanings and gurglings around the rock. The waves sparkled with phosphorescent light, and showed far-off, unearthly flashes, where they rolled over reefs that gradually lifted themselves as the tide went out.

Bess no longer strayed across to the other side of the island, but kept close to her cousin.

Randolph saw that she was getting nervous, and was manly enough not to blame her. He knew very well that the best cure for such a feeling was action.

"Bess," said he carelessly, as he wound his line in, "I'm going to dress these fish; and, while I'm doing it, I wish you'd take up a few handfuls of mussels and snails. We'll have a good clam-bake by and by."

"It won't take me long to do that," said Bess, beginning to work nervously. "I'll come over with you, I guess, as soon as I get enough."

"Thanks," said her cousin, "but I don't want your company just yet, Bess. Fish-cleaning isn't the nicest work in the world ; and besides, there's another job I want done right off."

"What's that, Ran ?"

"It's blowing up cold to-night, and we must arrange a sort of bulwark to keep the wind off. I got the idea from seeing some barnyards down on the Cape last year."

"Why, there's nothing to build it of!"

"Seaweed. Gather all you can, from the top layer, where a good deal of it has been dried, and comes off easy. The bigger heap you get, the better. I'll finish these prickly fellows up, and help you in a few minutes."

Bessie set to work, rather unwillingly it must be confessed, while Randolph went over to a convenient tide-pool to dress the fish.

The mussel-shells were sharp, and scratched her fingers ; the seaweed was slimy, and required hard pulling to detach it from the rocks. Still she found herself getting warmed up, and interested in the size of the pile she should make before her comrade returned.

There was a good mound of rock-weed well up on the ledge, as he appeared through the foggy dusk.

"Hullo!" he called out cheerily. "That's splendid, Bess! You remind me of a sort of marine Maud Muller, —

> "A mermaid, on a foggy night,
> Pulled up kelp with all her might."

"Only it isn't kelp, Ran," laughed Bess, breathing hard from her efforts.

"Poetical license, my dear. Rock-weed has one syllable too much; and you'll admit that *fucus vesiculosus* is out of the question!"

"You've got hold of Sue's seaweed book," cried Bess merrily. "I don't believe you'd ever heard of a *vesicul* — what is it? — a week ago."

"You have one great advantage over Maud Muller," remarked Randolph. "I can't conveniently 'ride off,' like the judge, no matter how saucy you are. I must decline to go into the question of the date of my Al — algæan acquirements."

"Why don't you say Algæ — braic?" laughed Bess, who had by this time quite recovered her spirits.

"Suppose you refrain from scoffing at me, Miss Percival, and assist in fortifying the camp?"

" How do you want it done? Where shall I take hold?"

Randolph took a handful of seaweed, and marked out a rude semicircle, enclosing their shelter. The line was only broken at the head of the arch, where space was left for a fire.

" There, make a long mound right round there. You might leave another little opening next the rock, to go in at, before we lock up for the night."

"Aren't you going to work too?"

" I'm going to get more seaweed. There isn't half enough here."

The rampart grew rapidly, until it was nearly three feet high. The slant of the rock carried away the drippings from the weed. Bessie stepped into the little enclosed area, and felt the comfort of the new wall immediately.

It was now eight o'clock, and quite dark. Healthy young folks, as they were, both began to look forward to supper.

Randolph kindled a fire, musing over the bits of drift-wood as he did so.

"Here's a shingle, from some coastwise schooner loaded with lumber. Look at that, — part of a boat's rail. What a story it could tell! Burns

well, don't it? Hullo, here's half an oar! Pretty
well worn out; been in a good many stormy seas,
I'll warrant."

He was about to throw it on the fire, when Bess
stopped him.

"It does seem a shame to burn it, though I
don't know what else we can do with it on this
rock."

"Oh, well, it'll keep till morning!" said Randolph, throwing it aside. "It'll make a good
pitchfork for your hay; or a flag-staff, to hail
passing vessels with."

The fire crackled and blazed up brightly. It
was a good fairy before; it was nothing less than
a blessed spirit now. The light shone into their
little shelter, giving it a cosey and homelike appearance. Its warmth, too, was grateful. Randolph placed the two big pieces of joist at the
back, one on the other, so that the heat radiated
directly into "Camp Trust."

"Not so bad, is it?" said Randolph, stepping in
through the opening, and taking his place beside
Bess. "We must wait a while for the coals to
burn down. Then we'll roast our shell-fish in the
ashes."

They talked a little at first; then sat there, looking at the fire, and listening to the murmuring
waves that seemed gathering about the island and
asking one another questions, — what this strange
fire and the two human beings meant by appear-
ing in their midst; and, as now and then one
and another voice would be heard, hoarser and
louder than the rest, whether it would not be
well to make a rush (as they had often done in
days past), and dash clean over Mingo, sweeping
away these frail creatures, with their puny shelter,
into the black depths of ocean.

Then the walls of seaweed would rise firm and
strong in the firelight, sending sweet, briny odors
in on the cool night breeze; and the fire itself
would blaze up brightly, and fling back a laugh at
the hungry, prowling pack outside; until these
very waves ceased to be terrible, and to Bess,
looking out timidly over her rampart at the white,
hurrying creatures, they seemed like a flock of
sheep, all obeying the Great Shepherd, and
anxious, not to destroy His child, but to lick her
hand and guide her back to home and safety as
soon as the world should have finished its sleep,
and waked up again into a sunny to-morrow.

The supper, it must be confessed, was not an entire success. The mussels and snails obstinately refused to "do," and the few that yielded at last were "about as big as baked beans," as Randolph observed, in tones of such disgust that Bess went off into the merriest of laughs. It was fortunate that they had dined late and plentifully. They ate the last of their biscuit, and, with such of the shell-fish as proved edible, managed to satisfy their hunger.

They made the meal last as long as they could; for, notwithstanding the comfort of fire and shelter, they could not help dreading the long, cold night. It was nearly ten o'clock before they began to fairly settle themselves for the seven hours of darkness yet to come. Randolph was building up the fire as economically as was consistent with a reasonable degree of warmth, when he was startled by an exclamation from Bess.

"Look overhead, Ran."

He looked. A star!

"The fog is going, Bess; we shall be all right in the morning! Somebody will come the first thing, when they see our flag of distress."

Star after star. The fog drifted away to the

south. And now a new glory came into the sky. The moon, nearly at the full, began to shine dully through the mists, brighter and brighter, — like a dead face coming to life, — until at last it shone out gloriously, transfigured with light.

Bess had stepped outside the wall of the camp, and stood by Randolph's side, clinging to his arm, her eyes wide open, drinking in the beauty of the scene.

In ten minutes more the sky was clear from east to west; a line of moonlight quivered over the dark sea as if He had walked upon it once more, and brought peace and light into the night.

Every rock, reef, and island stood out sharply. Shag and its neighboring ledges seemed like old friends, long absent.

Beyond lay the dark outlines of their own dear home-island, where hearts were beating anxiously for them.

As Randolph looked wistfully over toward the camp, he felt the girl's grasp tighten on his arm.

She pointed off toward the mouth of the channel between Mingo and Shag.

Randolph himself could not control a sudden start.

Half hidden in the water, some dark object was making its way slowly toward them.

"What can it be, Ran?"

He could feel her hand tremble as she asked the question which he could not answer.

It was far too large for a seal; that had been his first thought. It might have been a small whale, such as have been seen in those waters; but too much of its back was out of water. Could it be a walrus or sea-lion, straying down from the far-off shores of Labrador?

Randolph could think of nothing else, and his heart sank as he realized his feeble means of defence, should the huge beast attack them. He bade Bess step inside the little bulwark; then, grasping the fragment of the oar firmly, he awaited the approach of the strange visitor, whose character and movements were rendered more obscure by a light cloud that just then drifted across the face of the moon.

As yet, the creature had made no noise. Would it pass them without discovering their presence?

On it came, turning from side to side, with an odd, uncertain motion.

CHAPTER XIV.

LEFT BEHIND.

KITTIE, Pet, and Susie had planned for a quiet forenoon by themselves, gathering and arranging seaweeds, botanizing in a small way, and, in general, having one of those good "talks" which girls love, and which are always easier and more satisfactory when all are engaged in some light occupation.

You might not have thought it a "light occupation" to scramble over those rocks, and jump mimic crevasses, and tumble into rose-bushes, and snatch rare clumps of seaweed out of the water, darting back with a shriek of fright and fun, as a great wave came gambolling clumsily around the corner of the nearest rock. One would have supposed, I say, that the girls would have had plenty to occupy their minds as well as hands and feet, without any further topic.

But, dear me, those three Boston young ladies chattered like — schoolgirls, every moment.

"Where *do* you expect to go, Pet, after you leave the Shoals?" asked Kittie, at one time, emerging breathlessly from a leafy ravine into which she had half tumbled, half jumped.

"I don't know; the mountains, perhaps. Were you ever there, Susie?"

"At the mountains? Oh, no! I mean to go some time, though."

"Crawford's is just lovely."

"That's so," declared Kittie. "I wish we could all go there together. Perhaps next year we can make our plans to."

"And walk up the Mount Washington bridle-path!"

Susie listened wistfully, but said nothing.

"Girls, I see a little place down between those rocks where I know there must be some of those fine seaweeds, — the kind Susie got out there when the tide came in."

Pet jumped from one rock to another, and reached the coveted spot first.

"Oh, look!" She held up a handful of the beauties. True, they were rather stringy, but

they would unfold into loveliness as soon as they
were placed in a·basin.

"How queer it must have been," remarked
Susie, "when there were no flowers nor trees in
the world, — nothing but just seaweeds! Mr.
Percival was telling us about it the night before
he went back to Boston."

"Do you suppose it really was so? What a
dreary sight!"

"I don't know. After bare rocks, even seaweed
must have been a comfort."

"'A comfort'? O Susie, do you think what
you're saying? Just as if"—

"I know what you mean, Pet. And I believe it
was a comfort to God when He was through with
the firmaments and things, and got to seaweeds;
and it's not a bit wicked to think so. Don't
the Bible say that "He saw that it was good'?"

"I don't — know. I never thought of it that
way before. It don't seem just right to think of
Him taking comfort and being pleased with these
little things."

Pet spoke half under her breath, as if frightened
at the open manner in which she referred to her
Father in heaven.

"Don't you believe He's ever pleased?."

"Oh, of course it pleases Him to have us repent " —

"But wouldn't it be dreadful to think that He never was happy except when somebody was repenting? I couldn't take any comfort in flowers nor clouds, nor any thing, unless I thought He did too. Don't you know how pleased we always were, when we were children, to have our father or mother look at pictures with us, or hold our dolls and talk to them? It made them seem twice as nice. And I believe God loves to look at these things with us, just that way. Of course He could get along without them; but He *must* see that they're lovely, and if they're lovely He can't help loving them, just because He *is* God."

Susie's eyes shone as she turned eagerly to her companions; then she flushed a little to think how earnestly she had spoken.

"Of course," she added modestly, "I've no right to speak so, as if I really knew any thing about it. Only that's what grandmother thinks. She and I have often talked about it Sunday afternoons."

"Your grandmother is beautiful!" said Pet

enthusiastically. "I loved her the minute I saw
her. If I could only be like her, when I am an
old lady!"

"It's because she has always tried to make
other folks happy," said Susie, pleased to have
her friend speak so warmly. "She's all the time
doing something for somebody."

"Whenever I'm at your house," put in Kittie,
"she knits right along while she talks."

"Yes, mittens and stockings. She can knit in
the dark, or with her eyes shut, just as well as
in broad daylight. And oh, Kittie, when you're
sick!"

"Tell me about it."

"Why, she just goes in and out of the room
easy, — but not as if she was creeping on tiptoes,
that always makes me nervous, — and sits down
by you and holds your hand. Her hands are
always so cool and refreshing! And she fixes
little dishes of broth and toast in old-fashioned
ways, and makes them seem nice. And oh, her
aprons!"

"Aprons?"

"She always wears a kind of soft, fade-y apron.
I remember when I had typhoid-fever, two years

ago, and was over the worst of it, but very weak,
grandmother was holding me up to drink some
tea, and my head leaned over against her. The
minute my cheek touched that soft, quiet, old
apron, I was, somehow, so comforted that I
cried, just as hard as I could, and clung to her;
while she just kept on stroking my hair, — it had
got all hot and tumbled, you know; and pretty
soon I sat up and drank my tea, and then dropped
back on the pillow and had such a refreshing little
sleep."

Susie's eyes were shining again, and so were
two other pairs, blue and brown.

"I'll tell you what, girls," Susie concluded, with
a little loving tremble in her voice, "folks talk
about having angel wings hovering over them,
and all, — and it's lovely, too, to dream of that, —
but when I think of an angel that I could go to in
trouble, — next to the One who gave me grandmother, — I can't imagine one with a face dearer
than hers, or any wings or feathers so soft and
comforting to hide my face in, as that apron, with
the two hands smoothing my hair."

Before long, the girls concluded they had seaweed enough, and started slowly back toward

camp. But many were the sweet hinderances that delayed their feet. Now it was a whole bough of fluttering wild-roses, pink as the heart of a sea-shell; now a handful of long streamers hung with tiny trumpets, full of the morning glory they were named for.

In one of the seldom-visited spots on the higher part of the island, they started up the sandpipers, and soon were directed to the nest by their plaintive cries.

No wonder the birds had been distressed by Tom's visit to their home on the night of his arrival at Duck Island. One of God's every-day miracles had since been performed in that little nest, and the sandpipers had been expecting it to happen.

For when Kittie cautiously parted the long, coarse grass, and peered into the shadow of the rock, she no longer saw four spotted eggs, but four throbbing lives. Hardly any thing to be noted, as yet, but yellow, gaping mouths and little skinny bodies; but birds, nevertheless, with tiny sprouts of wings.

The girls answered the sandpipers' whistles with cries of delight; then softly withdrew.

On reaching camp they found their aunt asleep.
Bess and Randolph were nowhere in sight.

"Let's float the weeds, and arrange them up in
the tent," suggested Susie. "It will be real nice
and cool up there."

The girls tiptoed into camp, out again, and over
the rocks to the tent, bearing the pail of sea-mosses,
a book or two, a basin, and a pressing apparatus,
consisting of sheets of blotting-paper between
two boards, and a few pieces of old cotton cloth.

"See the herb-Robert," said Pet, as they took
their places just at the mouth of the tent.

"Yes, it grows all about these islands. What
pretty little pink blossoms!"

Kittie said nothing, but seemed struck with
a sudden thought.

"You two go on with your seaweeds," she said
with a business-like air. "I've got a little writing
to do."

"Why, I thought you'd answered all your
letters!"

Kittie pursed up her lips in a funny way, but
made no reply.

The girls set about their task in earnest. It
was delicate work, you may be sure.

First, they placed the mosses in a basin of clean, fresh water, and moved them about gently, to cleanse them from sand and other impurities.

They had brought with them some cards of bristol board, trimmed to a uniform size. One of these was now placed under a floating "moss," and the base or root drawn out to the side or corner it was to occupy. It needed Susie's steady hand to lift the card slowly to the surface, in such a way that the water ran off on all sides.

And now came the hardest part of all. I mean the adjustment of the exquisitely delicate branches and thread-like sprays in their proper positions. Often they had to dip the card again, to "float" the moss to the right spot. Sometimes it would take almost half an hour for a single specimen, while the next would be mounted in five minutes.

"How do you dry them?" asked Pet, who was delighted with this new occupation.

"I'll show you."

Susie laid down one of her large sheets of blotting-paper, and upon this her cards with the plants up. Then, lying directly on the speci-mens, she placed a piece of cotton, which had been kept smooth. On this another piece of blotting-paper; then more cards, more cotton, and so on. The whole was placed between two thin pieces of pine board, deposited in an out-of-the-way spot where they would not be disturbed, and a good-sized rock laid on them.

The only serious obstacle to the progress of this industry, it should be related, was Solomon, who from the outset was extremely interested in every step of the operation.

When the girls took their places in the tent-door, he followed waggingly, and, waiting until they were seated, accepted the invitation which a dog infers from the absence of a rebuff, and took his place beside them, the tip of his tail still vibrating from its last wag. When the mosses were placed in the basin, he evidently debated within himself whether they could be preparing a new dish, of which he might ere long be invited to partake; when Pet floated the specimens, and Susie lifted them carefully, he tipped his head over very much on one side, and stopped panting for a whole minute, so absorbed was he in the process; and he fain would have assisted in the final operations, with paw and nose, had his services not been most earnestly declined.

Just as the girls were gathering up their apparatus for a return to camp, Kittie re-appeared, flushed and radiant. Without a word, she flung down a sheet of note-paper in Susie's lap, and made a little pretence of going away, but plainly couldn't.

"Why, it's poetry!" said Susie, in some surprise. "Have you been copying all this time? Who is it for? Who wrote it, — Lowell?"

A queer, half-inarticulate sound from Kittie checked her questions, and made her look round sharply.

"Why, — Kit Percival, — you didn't write it *yourself!*"

Kittie nodded several times.

"What, our little girl writin' poetry!"

"O aunt Puss, have you waked up? You'll laugh, I know. Do give it back, Sue."

"Land!" said Mrs. Percival, "I'm not so terrible as all that. Read it aloud, Susie. — Solomon, keep off my gown!"

Susie glanced at the young authoress for permission, and, not being forbidden, read as follows: —

CONTENT.

"Little herb-Robert, what makes you so pink?
 The elder is taller and whiter."
"The sun came along, and — what do you think? —
 He kissed me, and so I grew brighter."

"Grasshopper, why are you merry to-day?"
 "I always am glad, if you please, sir,
Because I can hop on the clover and hay,
 Nor have to fly up in the trees, sir."

"Seaweed, poor creature! you're left high and dry;
 The tide has gone out; you are dying."
"Ah, no! I am sure 'twill come back by and by.
 I shall live, never fear; I'll keep trying."

"Song-sparrow, how can you sing all the day?"
 "Sweet food to my young I am bringing;
And when I am working for them, in this way,
 Of course I can never *help* singing."

"Child, leave the hot, dusty roadside, and come."
 "I'd go, for I know that you love me;
But, please, I had rather stay here, near my home,
 For papa's in there, just above me."

"Why, Kittie!" cried Pet, as Susie concluded,
"it's beautiful! How pretty that is about the
child in the street!"

"Pretty!" thought Kittie, and her heart sank,

as she saw that one, at least, of her auditors had entirely missed what she meant by the last verse. Pet had not yet thought deeply enough to understand; but Susie did, as Kittie saw a moment after, by the look in her eyes. As for aunt Puss, she just put her arms around the girl, and kissed her.

"I want to send that to grandmother," said Susie quietly. "Will you let me copy it?"

"Why, I'll be glad to, if you really care!" said Kittie, delighted.

"I do care."

Just then Mrs. Percival looked back over the island, and discovered the fog.

"I do declare," said she, "it's goin' to be a real overcast day. I hope 'twont rain before night."

As yet, no suspicion of danger to her husband or the young people crossed her mind.

"I guess we might's well be getting dinner ready," she added. "They'll all be hungry from rowing."

An hour later, the girls were waiting rather impatiently for the absentees to return. Dinner was ready, there was nothing particular to do, and the fog made things rather dreary.

"I suppose they've got interested in something, and so keep on stayin'," said Mrs. Percival resignedly. "I should think Bess would remind her uncle, though, that the folks at home were waitin' dinner."

"Why, Bess didn't go with them, aunt!"

"Didn't she? Where is she, then?"

"Off with Randolph somewhere. Let's go up on the rocks and call them."

They ran out bareheaded, and shouted in a dozen keys, assisted by long howls from Solomon, who came in like an oboe, filling the pauses in the phrases of the girlish voices.

No answer. Out of breath, and a trifle uneasy, they returned to camp.

"You might's well sit right down and eat a little," said aunt Puss. "They may be rambling round over Appledore this minute. Like's not William's found somebody he knows at the hotel."

They went through the form of eating; but the meal dragged, and they were glad when it was over.

After the dishes were cleared away, Mrs. Percival sat down by the window with a book; the girls started for a walk, but were soon driven in-doors by rain.

They played cat's cradle, crocheted a little, read, wrote a letter or two, and so the afternoon wore slowly away. They had discovered that both row-boats were gone; and now, as night came on, they all began to be seriously alarmed.

Hours passed, supper was cooked, and a pretence made of eating it.

They took as much time as possible in clearing up afterward.

By ten o'clock, they were almost too frightened to speak; a very little for themselves, very much for the rest of the party.

Unfortunately for their peace of mind, the conversation at last turned upon a terrible crime that had been committed not long before, under cover of darkness, on one of the islands. As they talked in low tones, the sense of loneliness and dread grew upon them minute by minute. They realized that they were four helpless, unprotected creatures, alone on this island, at midnight. They started at every sound. They were afraid to look at the little window, lest they should see evil eyes peering in.

Suddenly Kittie clutched Pet's arm, her breath coming quickly; a noise was heard on the beach outside. It sounded like a boat grating on the pebbles, where none of their party ever landed. The next indication of strangers was unmistakably a soft tread cautiously approaching the camp.

The dog pricked up his ears, sprang to his feet, and moved toward the door, not barking, but growling as if half in fear. The steps drew nearer, nearer.

C

CHAPTER XV.

THE ESCAPE.

WE left the two castaways on Mingo, at a little before midnight, watching with nervous apprehension the strange object coming toward them past the shoreward end of Shag.

There was something in its movements that they could not understand. It made no wake in the water, nor splashing noise of any kind, as a swimming animal would have done.

It was now hardly a hundred yards distant from their island. Bess was thoroughly frightened, but said nothing. Randolph never took his eyes from the creature.

At that moment, blessed relief, the cloud passed from before the moon, and let its face shine upon them once more. As the silvery light poured down over rock and wave, Bess uttered a cry of mingled astonishment and delight.

"Ran, Ran, it isn't alive at all! It's a great log, or something, floating."

"Better than that, Bess. It's our own boat, drifting out with the tide. If it will only come within reach!"

They sprang down toward the water's edge, as eager for the approach of the visitor as they had been for its departure a moment before. It was bottom-side up, just as they had seen it float out of sight that afternoon, after it had capsized in the breakers.

As it drifted toward them with the strong ebb tide, it became plain that it would not go within twenty feet of Mingo.

"I could swim," said Randolph, half to himself. But Bess cried out against that.

"What's the use?" she said. "We shall be taken off in the morning, anyway, and there's no need of your risking your life just to save a few hours. See how deep and black the water looks, and how the tide runs!"

While she was speaking, a plan came into her comrade's head. He hurriedly drew out his fish-line and began to unroll it, giving Bess the end, that it might not get tangled. The line was fully five fathoms, or thirty feet, long.

Next he took out his pocket-knife, and partly opened the large blade, which had a double spring, holding it firm half-way. It was one of those handy knives with a dozen queer blades and contrivances in the back and sides. Without difficulty he tied the line fast to the butt of the handle, by passing around a little notched socket into which a gimlet fitted. As he held up the line, the knife hung from the end of it like a letter L, or a huge *square* fish-hook.

"Now, Bess, let me have the reel. Here goes!"

The boat was almost abreast the bluff where they stood.

Randolph swung his knife once, twice, and flung it out. It dropped beyond the wherry. If it would only catch on the gunwale, all would be well.

Slowly he pulled in. There was no resistance beyond the friction of the line over the bottom of the boat. At a favorable moment he gave a little jerk, hoping the point of the blade would be toward him, and catch.

Alas, it came slipping over the smooth boards, and plunged into the water on this side of the boat, which quietly kept on its way toward the sea!

"Couldn't you take a heavy block of wood?" suggested Bess hastily.

"It would float, or break the line. If I only had a small rock!"

But there was not a rock on the island of less than a ton's weight. The waves had swept its surface too often and too well.

It took careful manœuvring not to let the knife catch among the seaweed, or on the bottom. But Randolph succeeded in getting it in, and made another cast as quickly as he could.

The knife took out the whole length of the line, and fell short fully three feet.

" There's just one more chance," said he, pulling in as rapidly as he dared. "It may set in toward that north-east point a little. I'll try it."

He ran up on the rocks, and hurried to the point he had in mind. Beyond that was open ocean. If the boat once passed the gateway between the "Eastern Rocks" and Mingo, they probably would never see her again.

It was not an easy nor an altogether safe undertaking, to scramble round over those ledges by moonlight. The boy received two or three ugly bruises; once he slipped and almost went overboard. But he reached the point just ahead of the boat, which now rose and fell on the long swell that came rolling in from outside.

Bess was beside him a moment later, and breathlessly watched the final trial.

Out shot the line, the knife-blade glittering at the end.

It settled over the boat. So far, all was well.

Then came a long half-minute of suspense, as Randolph hauled in gently. The line came smoothly enough for a moment; then its progress was checked. A gentle pull, and it tightened, while the boat turned perceptibly toward the rock.

"O Ran, it's coming!"

"Don't say a word, Bess. I expect to feel it slip every minute; and I don't dare to put a pound of strain on the line. The main point is to keep a steady pull on it, as if 'twas a big trout."

It was now hardly ten feet away. The hinder part of the boat began to swing round with the tide. In another moment the blade must slip.

Randolph pulled harder than he had before, and barely dodged the open knife as it came flying towards his head.

"Oh, she's gone!"

But the boy did not give up. That last jerk
had sent the boat's head up still nearer the rock.
He held on tightly, with his right hand, to a projecting point, and standing waist-deep in water,
reached out farther, farther, until the boat was
only six inches away, — four inches — one — and
his fingers rested on it. Ten seconds later, its
bows were grating against the rocks.

Randolph, meanwhile, was in a most uncomfortable situation; for the rise and fall of the
waves along the island, now left him almost
entirely out of water, now came swashing up
nearly to his shoulders.

He kept his grip on the rock, however, and feeling down under the bows of the wherry, got hold
of the painter, which he managed to pass to Bess;
after which manœuvre he was glad enough to climb
upon dry land once more.

" What do you mean to do now, Ran?" inquired
Bess anxiously.

" Well, first I'll tow the boat round to our
harbor."

" Aren't you going to tip it over, right-side-up."

" What's the use? The waves will capsize it
again. No, I'm going to take her round just as

she is, — let me have the rope, please, — and while I get just a trifle dry by the fire, *you* are to hold the wild steed, Bess. The painter's so long, you can stay up above the line of perpetual seaweed. Then I'll right the boat, and get the water out of her, while *you* toast yourself, up in Camp Trust."

"And then ?"

"Then we'll start for home."

"Why, you've no oars !"

"We'll take that broken one. Wait till you see me paddle like a Pawnee !"

The programme was faithfully carried out. The wherry was a light one, as I have said, and Randolph did not have much trouble in pulling it up on the slippery rock-weed, and emptying the water out of her.

They extinguished the fire, that no seaman might be misled by this unusual beacon, and bade good-by, with a certain feeling of sadness, to Camp Trust.

Randolph took his seat in the stern of the boat, after getting his cousin safely in, and pushing off. He had learned to paddle on the Maine lakes, and the little "castaway" rippled along merrily through the water.

They moved slowly against the tide ; but soon
they were out of the channel, and steering for
home. The wind had almost entirely died away,
and hardly a ripple broke the glassy surface of the
sea, on which the moonlight poured in a golden
flood.

As they approached Duck Island, Randolph
decided to land on the beach instead of near the
regular moorings, where the low tide and the
shadows of the bluffs might make it a dangerous
attempt.

The boat was easily beached, and made fast to
a big rock.

" Let's go up quietly," said Bess, "and see what
they're doing. There's a light in the hut now.
Do you suppose uncle Will is telling stories ? "

As they drew near, they heard a low growl.

" It's Solomon," whispered Bess. " That will
wake them, anyway. Let's knock."

A torrent of excited barks answered their tap.

They opened the door, and behold, four blanched
faces and shrinking forms !

" Why, aunt Puss, what's the matter ? Where's
uncle Will ? "

" And Tom ? And Bert ? "

"Randolph, is that you?" Mrs. Percival found voice at last, and, rushing forward, flung her arms around the boy's neck, with a sob, while the girls surrounded Bess.

Of course they had to tell their adventures, over and over. Aunt Puss insisted on the cast-aways eating a hot lunch, and it was past two o'clock when they began to realize that they were sleepy.

But now came another surprise. From the shore arose a cheery shout.

They rushed to the door, and saw the three "missing links," as Kittie, half laughing and half in tears, called them.

In the moonlit offing was the steam-yawl "Pin-afore," puffing away toward her moorings at Appledore.

A new set of adventures to be rehearsed, and a repetition of the Mingo episodes.

As for Mr. Percival's party, it seemed that just as they had given up all hope of reaching either the mainland or the island that night, the fog had cleared off, and shortly afterward the "Pinafore" was heard coming down the river.

She was hailed and boarded by the three

passengers, and stood off toward the Shoals with
the wherry in tow. She had been kept at Portsmouth by the fog, it seemed; but as Mr. Oscar
Laighton had come up in her on business, and
was anxious to be at the hotel in good season next
morning, they had decided to run out by moonlight. By making a slight détour, the little
steamer had obligingly brought the campers close
up to Duck Island, and they had landed in their
own wherry.

Worn out with watching, talking, and listening,
as well as with the exertions of the day and night,
they all "turned in" at last; nor did a single
member of "Camp Kelp" (except a certain four-
legged one) awake before ten o'clock the next
forenoon.

CHAPTER XVI.

STAR ISLAND.

IT can easily be imagined that but little sight-seeing was accomplished on the day following the fog. The sun shone out bright and clear, however; and Mr. Percival, with all three of the boys, did rouse themselves so far as to row over to Appledore for ice, fresh water, and the mail, in the course of the forenoon.

The trip was uneventful, saving a little excitement caused by Randolph's hat falling overboard, and its subsequent capture by Tom, who proudly raised it on the end of his oar.

In the mail were letters for all the party, and a book for Tom.

On being questioned as to his parcel, that young gentleman rather shamefacedly announced that it was a work on botany for which he had written to his father. To uncle Will, who was anxious to know what had induced the boy to send for such

a work, he said frankly, that he had thought over all they had talked of, that day at Appledore, and that he had determined to make a beginning. He had always had a sort of desire, he said, to be a doctor; and, while he might change his mind before leaving school and college, he meant to take one step in that path, — a step that could only lead to good, and not harm, in any case. He knew that an acquaintance with botany was a necessary part of a physician's education, and he had resolved to begin the study that very day.

"What do you think of the profession, uncle?" he asked rather anxiously, as he concluded.

"It's a noble one, my boy. You can do a great deal of good to body and soul."

"Soul?"

"Yes, indeed. A man will listen to his doctor when he won't have a minister under his roof. You won't have to 'preach.' It will be a word now and then, a suggestion, showing to whom you look yourself as to a Great Physician. O Tom, my boy, it makes my heart ache, sometimes, to see how doctors miss the chance of administering that medicine which the patient most needs! Of all men, a physician should be an earnest Christian, going about and healing the sick, as his Master did in Palestine."

"And what do you think of my beginning botany, sir?" Tom asked, after a moment of silence.

"A capital idea. You probably won't get far ahead in it this summer; but read thoroughly as far as you go, and carry your book into the field with you whenever you can."

"I mean to make a list of all the plants I can find the names of on Duck Island."

"Good! Come to me when you get puzzled, and perhaps I can help you. I used to know something about these things, though my botany is getting a little rusty now."

So Tom found a new occupation, and a fascinating one. It was astonishing how his list lengthened in that and the following day. Roses, bay, elder, herb-Robert, clover, morning-glories, vetchlings, golden rod (just budding), fleur-de-lis, and many others, he found and checked in his book.

The next day Mr. Percival proposed a visit to Star Island, with a circuit around to Londoner's on the way.

AT LONDONERS.

They took the sloop, with the wherry in tow, and the whole party went. They could not bear to be separated again.

The wind had blown up rather fresh from the east during the night; and, after making a little offing from camp toward the mainland, they were enable to run directly for Londoner's in an almost southerly course, some three miles distant.

Mr. Percival let a mackerel line and "jig" troll astern, and within a few minutes had three of the beautiful, glittering creatures in the bottom of the boat, — a welcome addition to the larder.

Off Appledore they met the "Pinafore," which saluted them with three whistles. A crowd of gay young people on board waved handkerchiefs, hats, and parasols, to which aunt Puss politely responded with a large blue umbrella.

Londoner curves like a half moon, with a harbor at the head of the crescent. The sloop anchored where she had plenty of water, and a landing was effected by means of the wherry.

There was one house on the island, occupied by a small family. The children — pretty, little rosy-cheeked girls, with bare feet, and tangled curls falling over their shoulders — shyly offered strings of shell, which were bought by the Percivals for mementos. Aside from the shells, the most remarkable feature of the island was its morning-glories, which grew in profusion over the rocks and down to high-water mark on the beach.

Embarking once more, our campers set sail for Star. To reach this island they had to beat up against the wind, which, having hauled a little towards the north, was almost dead ahead.

They were sailing along quietly enough, when, to everybody's astonishment, not to say conster-nation, the sloop gently came to a standstill, and evinced a disposition to lie down on its side.

"What on airth's the matter with the boat?" demanded Mrs. Percival, not fully realizing the peril of their situation.

"We're on Half-way Rock," replied her husband, and he proceeded to give orders rapidly.

"All back into the stern! We've only run up on the rocks a few feet, and the wind may take us off."

But the wind did not take them off, and the sloop careened still farther.

"Out into the wherry with me, boys. Change

the painter ; make fast. That's right ! Now, with a will, *pull!*"

Half-a-dozen powerful strokes, and they were rewarded by seeing the larger boat glide off back-ward, and ride easily once more.

She instantly fell off before the wind, and the boys scrambled on board to prevent an accident.

"It was inexcusable in me," said Mr. Percival, as they proceeded on their course once more. "Though I see that the spar that marks the ledge has dragged its anchor some distance from the most dangerous spot, still I ought to have remem-bered the rock, and given it a wide berth."

In due time they arrived at Star Island, and made fast to the wharf, out of the way of the large steamer which would soon be due from Portsmouth.

"Let's walk right up to the Oceanic," remarked Mr. Percival. "There are one or two people there whom I want to see. You young folks can be exploring, meanwhile. In twenty minutes we'll all walk over to the outer side of the island."

Aunt Puss said she would wait in the parlor. The rest walked about near the water, and at the appointed time Pet and Kittie were despatched to summon uncle Will.

They found him sitting on the broad piazza, nodding over a Boston paper. His green glasses, which he generally wore while walking round in a brilliant sun, gave him a very philosophical aspect; from which, it must be confessed, the broad straw hat detracted somewhat.

The girls whispered together, and decided not to disturb him; but he glanced up quickly, caught sight of the laughing faces, shook his finger at them, and quickly joined the party, bringing Aunt Puss with him as he came.

"Uncle Will is as hard as a weasel to catch napping," laughed Kittie, putting her arm affectionately through his.

They walked up over the steep rocks where the houses of Gosport had once been, and stopped to look at the little meeting-house that still bravely breasts the storms, and points upward, winter and summer.

"The first church on this spot was built of timbers from the wrecks of Spanish ships," Mr. Percival informed them, after consulting his book. "'It has since been burned and rebuilt twice,'" he read aloud. "'The last time it was damaged (by fire) was in 1826.'"

ON THE PIAZZA
OF THE
OCEANIC.

They stepped inside, and looked reverently at the straight-backed, sturdy little pews, and rude pulpit, where the words of the Ruler of the sea had been so often read and listened to. Much more of the history of the island and its early inhabitants uncle Will read, and told the young folks, as they sauntered slowly over the rocky meadow that lies between shore and shore.

When they reached the eastern cliffs, they found a grand sight awaiting them. The easterly wind had brought in a lively swell, and such a surf was already beating on the rocks as they never before had seen. The sky was still fair, but the gathering clouds and increasing wind all betokened a coming storm.

"What's that board for, nailed up against the rocks?" asked inquisitive Pet.

It was an inscription, in memory of Miss Underhill, a young school-teacher who used to come over to these cliffs when her work was done, each day, and look off at the ocean which stretched away before her for three thousand miles.

One day, as she was resting quietly there, a huge wave swept up to her, took her in its arms, and bore her to heaven.

The girls were saddened by the story, and were glad to leave the cliffs, at whose feet the waves were dashing now as then. They rambled about over the little island, visited a monument erected in memory of Capt. John Smith, who discovered these islands, and finally reached a historic gulch among the rocks at the north end of Star, already alluded to as " Betty Moody's Cave." Tom scrambled down into the "cave," followed by Bess, who never allowed herself to be outdone by her brother.

"Come, boys," said Mr. Percival, at length, with an anxious look at the sky; "we'd better be moving. There's a storm blowing up, and we want to be prepared for it."

They hurried back to the wharf, climbed aboard their boat, and stood out across the " roads " toward the north-west, between Star and Apple-dore.

A longer sail was before them than they knew. As soon as they passed out of the lee of the larger island, they struck the full force of the wind, which was now something more than a fresh breeze from the north-east, the exact direction in which they wanted to go.

"Why, William," exclaimed poor aunt Puss, gazing over toward Duck Island, "you're going right away from home!"

"Can't help it, Eunice. We must beat up a good two miles, against this wind. — Let her off a little!" he called out to Randolph, who was steering. "Give her a good full for stays. Now, *hard-a-lee!*"

Down went the helm, and up came the sloop into the wind. The girls screamed, laughed, and dodged to escape the boom. The big sail caught the wind, and slowly the sloop filled away again; this time heading directly out to sea, and taking the full force of the waves on the weather-bow. The water flew in sheets over the little forecastle, and down into the standing-room. Mr. Percival protected aunt Puss and the girls as well as he could, with tarpaulins and shawls; but they were well drenched before they scrambled up on the rocks of Duck Island an hour later.

The sloop was moored, as usual, in mid-channel; and the campers set busily to work preparing dinner, for it was now past two o'clock. Solomon, it was noticed, did not enter into the spirit

of the occasion, as was his wont, but seemed
disposed to sit in corners and meditate.   Kittie
suggested that it was probably a bad conscience,
and had to visit the sandpipers' nest before she
could assure herself to the contrary.   As there
was nothing particularly bad that Solomon could
do on the island but eat young sandpipers, his
sedate demeanor was laid to ill-health ; and they
decided to give him a very light dinner, whereat
his spirits sank still lower.

The sun had disappeared in a bank of clouds.
As yet, there was neither rain nor fog ; only an
utter absence of bright color in sea, sky, or land.
It seemed as if the very air was gray.   The
wind moaned around the little hut, and now and
then gave a tug at the tent near by, which boded
no good.

Uncle Will went out on the rocks and took
an observation.   When he came back, his face —
though by no means showing any alarm — was
decidedly grave.

"Girls," said he, "I remember your saying,
when you first came, that you wished you could
see a real storm at the Shoals.   You can set your
minds at rest on that point.   Before to-morrow

night, unless I am very much mistaken, you will be quite willing to see fair weather again. Randolph, Tom, Bert, come out with me, and help me take the sloop round to the south cove. She is dragging her anchor."

CHAPTER XVII.

CAMP KELP IN A STORM.

IT was no easy task to get safely aboard the
sloop, and navigate her around the dangerous
southerly point of the island. Ordinarily, she
would have been far safer in the little roadstead
between Duck and Shag; but the wind was
squally, and eddied round the northern reefs, so
as to send the sea rolling through the channel
in a fashion that both endangered her safety,
and made her extremely difficult to handle in
that narrow passage. They did not attempt to
hoist the sail which would have been unmanage-
able without a double reef, but, using the heaviest
oars, managed to row her out of danger, to her
new anchorage, where she was moored, stem and
stern, to make sure.

Returning in the larger wherry, Mr. Percival
and the boys landed on the beach, and pulled
the boat well up out of the reach of the waves;

which, however, were not likely to run high on
this side of the island, as the wind was. The
lighter boat had already been cared for.

By the time all this had been done, and several
big armfuls of drift-wood brought in under shelter,
it was nearly six o'clock. All were surprised to
see how soon darkness came on. The tide was
still running out, and would not turn much before
ten that night.

Attention was now directed afresh to the tent,
upon which the wind seemed to have especially
malevolent designs, — springing at it suddenly,
and shaking it as a terrier would a rat; then
becoming quiet, and a minute later rushing over
the rocks from a new quarter, with a headlong
force that would almost tear the canvas from the
ropes.

The boys strengthened it all they could, laying
large stones upon the edges of the canvas, adding
new ropes, and, in general, preparing for a night
attack.

At seven o'clock a light scud came in from the
east, and buried what dim ghost of daylight there
was left.

After supper the fire was replenished, and

the penetrating dampness of the wind made its
warmth most welcome. The Percivals found
themselves inclined to be silent, as they drew up
the various boxes and stools that constituted the
furniture of the hut, and sat in a half-circle,
gazing at the fire.

Only three days more of their stay remained ;
for I have given you but the main incidents,
and omitted any account of the long forenoons
and afternoons they had passed in walking about
the island, or rowing over the quiet waters that
surround it.

" When did Henry write that he was coming ? "
asked Mrs. Percival.

" Next Monday, — day after to-morrow," replied
uncle Will. " On Tuesday we must break camp,
if the wind doesn't do it for us before that," he
added, as a stronger gust than usual made the
timbers of the little hut shiver and creak.

The girls looked at each other, but said
nothing.

Solomon's uneasiness, which had been steadily
on the increase, now led him to get up and walk
about the room. Presently he snuffed at the
door, and whined a little. Bert opened it, and

the dog stepped out, then stopped, standing and looking over his shoulder in an uncertain way.

" Why, the dog 's half scared to death ! " exclaimed aunt Puss. " Look at his tail ! And he' s shivering from head to foot."   ·

" Come, Sol.   Poor fellow ! " called Tom coaxingly.

But nothing could induce the dog to step inside the door again.

" Hear the breakers ! " said Pet, in low tones. " They' ve never been so loud before."

The noise of their booming on the outside rocks filled the air.   The wind was blowing harder than ever ; and the rain was falling — or rather sweeping straight across the island — in a fine, dense drizzle.

" I hope no ship is within ten miles of here," said uncle Will solemnly.   " It's going to be a fearful night along the coast.   And the Shoals lie just out of the path of small Maine vessels."

They went into the hut again, and after a little more talk separated for the night.   The boys found it hard work to make their way over the few feet of intervening rough ground to the tent. It was pitch-dark, for a lantern could not be kept alight a moment.

Solomon consented, with evident misgivings and draggled fur, to share Tom's bed of straw; and the five inmates of the tent composed themselves to sleep.

Tom knew he would be stupid and headache-y on the next day if he staid awake much longer. He therefore conscientiously entered upon a series of experiments to encourage slumber.

He naturally began with that old device of watching imaginary waves break upon a sea-shore. But before long he found himself regulating their fall by the roar of the real breakers close at hand. This made them far too realistic, and that line of attack was abandoned. He now made a flock of sheep jump over a stone wall, in endless procession.

This might have soothed him in time, had not Solomon, as if by mind-reading he recognized the scene in Tom's brain, suddenly given a yelp; after which he settled down again, a little ashamed of himself, it seemed.

But that yelp put to flight not only every sheep in Tom's pasture, but every vestige of sleep in his wool-gathering wits.

He heard Randolph move uneasily beside him, and ventured to whisper, " Ran, you awake ? "

"Yes. Can't get asleep."

"No more can I. Let's creep out and get a breath of air."

The two boys, on emerging into the black, out-door night, found that they could now dimly see the white of the breakers; for the moon was up, though her face was hidden by clouds. Randolph shivered, as he and Tom leaned, arm in arm, against the wind.

"Isn't it funny," he remarked presently, "how it seems to rain for a minute, and then stop altogether? There, I got a real splash right in my face."

"I don't understand it a bit," gasped Tom, who had evidently received the same visitation. "It doesn't rain a drop now. Don't you believe we can get up on the rocks a little, so as to be within sight of the waves?"

As he spoke, there came a roar, like artillery, that seemed to shake the very island beneath them. A moment later a smart shower of water came slap against their faces.

"Whew! that isn't rain!" said Randolph.

"How do you know?"

"Because it's *salt*."

"You don't suppose the spray from the breakers flies clear over the island?"

"I do mean just that. I tell you, Tom, I wouldn't give much for a fellow's life on Mingo just now."

He got no further, for a blast of wind came sweeping over the ledges that fairly made them both stagger. Before he could speak again there came a tearing, ripping sound close beside them, mingled with wild outcries from Solomon, the flapping of canvas, and a series of energetic remarks in the combined voices of Bert and uncle Will.

The two outsiders sprang heedlessly through the darkness, and tumbled headlong upon the heaving, kicking, shouting mass that occupied the site of the tent.

The accession of the two boys did not diminish the confusion. They cried to those beneath, however, as well as they could for laughing, to be patient, and they should be extricated. Just as they raised one corner of the canvas, the wind came to their assistance, and, wrenching the tent bodily from the ground, bore it away triumphantly.

The whole affair was over so quickly that the four campers stood there in helpless bewilderment.

A fresh shower of spray soon admonished them to take action.

"Form a line!" shouted uncle Will, above the howling wind and the continuous roar of the breakers. "Bert, you stand nearest the hut, and pile up the things before the door as we pass them. Now, Tom, lively."

Each braced himself firmly against the wind, and handed the boxes and packages through the darkness to his neighbor, like an old-fashioned fire department. In ten minutes the ledge was as bare as it had been on the first day of their arrival. The wind swept away every wisp of straw.

"Now hand the boxes in. Randolph, you and Bert step inside. Look out, Eunice, you'll be blown away!" For by this time the five inmates of the hut were crowding to the open door, and peering over each other's shoulders, in a vain attempt to make out what was going on outside.

"Are you all safe?" demanded aunt Puss anxiously.

"All here, and all safe," answered her husband.

"That's right, boys. Pass 'em along. Randolph, pile them up in a corner inside there."

"Where's Solomon?" Tom's voice was heard asking.

Nobody had seen him or heard his bark since the tent went to sea.

They whistled and called, but no Solomon appeared.

"He must have tumbled into the water, off those high rocks. You know he never knew how to take care of himself in the waves."

Poor dog! Tom felt his loss keenly. He had sometimes felt that Sol understood him better than anybody else did. And every wag of his honest tail, and glance of his eye, had spoken his devotion to his master.

Mr. Percival now gave orders that all should be quiet, and, if possible, get a little sleep. He pinned up shawls, with Kittie's aid, so as to give the girls something over half the hut, including the fire end. Stretching themselves out as comfortably as the crowded space allowed, the whole party slept in fitful naps, and in the intervals listened to the boom of the breakers, and the wild, moaning rush of the wind around their little refuge.

SOLOMAN.

Morning came at length. One by one the boys rose stiffly from their hard resting-place, and sought the door. Once outside, they forgot the discomforts of the night. Never had they seen, or even imagined, such a sight.

The girls presently joined them ; and, as it was not now raining, they all made their way, fighting against the wind, to the highest point of the island. For miles in every direction the sea was a leaping, boiling cauldron of foam. The waves came charging in from the open ocean, in ranks and regiments, to plunge madly at the little island, which now seemed hardly sufficient to afford foothold to the awestruck group of campers huddled together upon its gray ledges.

The thunder of the breakers was so great as to render conversation impossible ; and it was only by gestures, and shouting at the top of their voices, that they could communicate with each other.

Randolph touched Bess on the arm, and pointed to Mingo Even as she looked, there was no Mingo there, — only a white mound of foaming water. A moment later the rock emerged from the wave, only to cast another huge waterspout into the air. It was the same with Shag and the Eastern Rocks.

The girls·soon found, that, if they wanted to have a dry stitch upon them, they must seek some shelter. For not only was the air full of flying spray, but long ropes of yellowish foam continually drifted across the island, coiling about and drenching whatever they struck.

"Back to the house!" shouted uncle Will.

As they turned, they could see their little sloop riding at anchor in the lee of the island, but even there rising, falling, rolling to one side and the other, as if in utter distress. The walls of the hut were dripping with salt spray, and coated with bunches and strings of foam.

Tom called again for Solomon, but at length reluctantly gave it up, and followed the rest into camp.

Preparing breakfast was a difficult task, as the fire was half the time blazing and smoking right out into the room, and the other half leaping up the chimney until nothing was left but glowing brands in the fireplace.

The young people found it impossible to stay within doors, and protecting themselves as well as they could with waterproofs and cloaks, crouched in sheltered situations side by side, and silently watched the wonderful scene before them. By noon the gale was at its height, and Mr. Percival was seriously afraid the hut would go down before it. The sloop, too, was evidently in great danger; but nothing could be done to relieve the strain on its moorings, at which it tugged and jerked like a frightened horse.

At about eleven o'clock in the forenoon, a shout from Tom called their attention to a terrible sight. About two miles to windward a full-rigged ship was laboring in the heavy sea. Her top rigging was gone, only one poor rag of a sail set, and, pitiful sight, the American flag fluttered in the fierce wind, *union down.*

"Signal of distress," said uncle Will, with almost a groan; "and we can't lift a hand to help her!"

In ten minutes more she was out of sight, driving directly toward the south-west before the wind. They heard afterward that she went ashore on the rocks near Marblehead, a total wreck; but that every man on board was taken off alive, through the splendid heroism of the Life-saving crew at that station.

At noon Mr. Percival did not dare to build a fire in the hut. The wind scattered the blazing coals from the fireplace in such a way as to place the floor in constant danger of catching; and it was plain to all, that, if the flames once started, the hut and its contents would be doomed. Accordingly they had to satisfy themselves with a cold meal, looking over their shoulders nervously, as they ate, every time a blast of wind shook the slight framework about them.

" Bess," remarked uncle Will, "are you satisfied with the reality of your storm ? "

"O uncle, I never dreamed of any thing so grand ! "

" But I think we wouldn't mind if it would go down a little now," added Pet rather soberly.

"I wish it would keep on so for a week ! " exclaimed Susie, clasping her hands in ecstasy as an unusually loud roar from the surf fell on their ears, and the walls of the hut creaked and groaned like the timbers of a ship at sea. "Oh, I could never be tired of it ! "

But storms must have an end; and by six o'clock a long, golden flash shot across the water

from the western sky. The waves still hurled
themselves in tremendous masses upon the outer
reefs, and flung their white arms high over Shag
and Mingo ; the wind still blew hard, shifting to
the north, and gradually toward the west ; but the
force of the gale was plainly abating.

By half-past seven its violence was not nearly
so great ; the sky was clear, and the girls could
keep their footing on the ledges with some degree
of comfort.

Tom was exploring the shore near the hut,
when he heard a low whine.

How he did start ! The noise seemed to come
from the direction of the smaller wherry, which
was hauled up above high-water mark.

He hurried to the boat, and there, curled up in
a drenched, piteous little heap, but springing to
his feet at sight of his master, and converting
himself into one continuous, vibrating wag, was
the lost Solomon !

Tom hugged him, all dripping as he was, and
cried a little into his dingy fur, before leading him
back to the hut, and exhibiting him to the aston-
ished inmates.

" He was afraid the hut would fall, and so he

took refuge in the boat after trying his best to make us come too," said uncle Will, patting the honest forehead.

"Land, he must be hungry, poor fellow!" And aunt Puss bustled about to prepare a dish of good things for the dog.

Solomon bore his honors meekly; and Randolph declared he ever after wore an additional look of wisdom, based on his sagacious action that night.

Of what use would it be to tell of the few remaining hours of their stay on Duck Island?

It is better to leave our friends in Camp Kelp, with Pet's golden hair still tossing in the wind, above the sunny ledges of the lonely island; Tom poring over its floral treasures; Susie taking into her very soul the beauty of God's sea and sky; the sandpipers rejoicing that they and their young had been sheltered by the rock in the tempest; and the troubled ocean obeying its Master's command as of old, "Peace, be still!"

With Tom's father added to their number on the second day after the gale, — no boat could land there for the next twenty-four hours, — the party was complete.

During the last day mementos were gathered, and carefully packed for home.

Uncle Will examined the curious rocks described by Susie, and pronounced the tiny dark points which were scattered all over its surface, firmly imbedded in the solid granite, to be garnets. A few fragments of the ledge were knocked off, but the little stones were never taken from their natural setting.

It is just before sunset. To-morrow morning they will turn their faces toward home ; uncle Will and his gentle wife returning to the Maine pines, the rest to Boston. The Percivals expect to visit the White Mountains in August. At this moment they can see the shadowy form of Mount Washington rising among the clouds ninety miles away.

They are seated on the little knoll where they had gathered when they landed, a fortnight before. Their faces would be sad at the thought of parting, did not the gladness and beauty about them shine in their hearts and their eyes.

In the bay, just below, the rock-weed lifts and droops with the soft touch of the waves, and long streamers of kelp, turning their dark sides toward the west, glisten in the slant, golden rays of sunlight. The breeze blows softly from the land; now with warm scents of field and wood, now with the salt breath of the ocean.

All around the little island the sea sighs, murmurs, sparkles in the last gleam of the setting sun, and sinks to sleep.

THE END.